Summer Sunset CONFIDENTIAL

JF
Morgan, Melissa J.
Sunset

JUN 26 2009

MID-CONTINENT PUBLIC LIBRARY
Smithville Branch
205 Richardson
Smithville, MO 64089   **SM**

WITHDRAWN
FROM THE RECORDS OF THE
MID-CONTINENT PUBLIC LIBRARY

by Melissa J. Morgan

Grosset & Dunlap

GROSSET & DUNLAP
Published by the Penguin Group
Penguin Group (USA) Inc., 375 Hudson Street, New York, New York 10014, USA
Penguin Group (Canada), 90 Eglinton Avenue East, Suite 700,
Toronto, Ontario M4P 2Y3, Canada
(a division of Pearson Penguin Canada Inc.)
Penguin Books Ltd., 80 Strand, London WC2R 0RL, England
Penguin Group Ireland, 25 St. Stephen's Green, Dublin 2, Ireland
(a division of Penguin Books Ltd.)
Penguin Group (Australia), 250 Camberwell Road, Camberwell, Victoria 3124, Australia
(a division of Pearson Australia Group Pty. Ltd.)
Penguin Books India Pvt. Ltd., 11 Community Centre, Panchsheel Park,
New Delhi—110 017, India
Penguin Group (NZ), 67 Apollo Drive, Rosedale, North Shore 0632, New Zealand
(a division of Pearson New Zealand Ltd.)
Penguin Books (South Africa) (Pty.) Ltd., 24 Sturdee Avenue,
Rosebank, Johannesburg 2196, South Africa

Penguin Books Ltd., Registered Offices:
80 Strand, London WC2R 0RL, England

If you purchased this book without a cover, you should be aware that this book is stolen property.
It was reported as "unsold and destroyed" to the publisher, and neither the author nor the publisher
has received any payment for this "stripped book."

The scanning, uploading, and distribution of this book via the Internet or via any other means
without the permission of the publisher is illegal and punishable by law. Please purchase only
authorized electronic editions and do not participate in or encourage electronic piracy of
copyrighted materials. Your support of the author's rights is appreciated.

Text copyright © 2009 by Grosset & Dunlap. All rights reserved. Published by Grosset & Dunlap,
a division of Penguin Young Readers Group, 345 Hudson Street, New York, New York 10014.
GROSSET & DUNLAP is a trademark of Penguin Group (USA) Inc. Printed in the U.S.A.

Library of Congress Control Number: 2008039441

ISBN 978-0-448-44989-0   10 9 8 7 6 5 4 3 2 1

MID-CONTINENT PUBLIC LIBRARY - BTM

3 0003 00903231 7

MID-CONTINENT PUBLIC LIBRARY
Smithville Branch
205 Richardson
Smithville, MO 64089

SM

One

Cassie felt as if she were surfing. But she knew she wasn't. In fact, when she looked down she could see her white flip-flops trudging over the sand, and she could hear them click-clacking against her heels—but it didn't *feel* like she was walking at all. It was like the earth was moving beneath her and she was somehow managing to remain upright. As if she was gliding.

There's nothing like kissing the boy you're crazy about to make you lose all sensation in your legs.

Of course, she and Micah hadn't actually *kissed* kissed. They almost kissed. She'd puckered up, closed her eyes, and felt the warmth of his breath. But just before their lips came together, they were interrupted. By Danica, of all people.

As disappointed as she was, Cassie had to

admit to the teensiest amount of relief, too. She hadn't been prepared for the kiss to happen, and she would have appreciated a little heads-up. Because the total lame reality of the situation was this: She really didn't have much experience in the whole making-out department.

What if she was bad at it? What if Micah *had* locked lips with her and then discovered she was terrible at it?

The floaty feeling of having shared airspace with Micah was now beginning to fade. Cassie gradually became aware of the slidy sand beneath her shoes, and the itchy granules sticking to the recently applied sunblock on her legs.

She did a quick mental recap: Micah liked her, and that was good. He wanted to kiss her, also good. But she had zero history with boyfriends and hardly any kissing experience (just party games and friendly pecks on the cheek). And that was bad. Sad, scary bad.

Micah, she knew, had had girlfriends. Maybe even lots of them. Including Danica, the smokin' hot alpha female of Camp Ohana.

And oh, right—they had just left together for

a big surf competition in Oahu, where they would spend two nights in a hotel.

More bad.

Of course they had separate rooms and chaperones, but it didn't take Einstein to figure out that hotel plus ex-girlfriend plus honeymoon capital of the world equaled big reason to worry.

Cassie came to a stop. Now the light, gliding sensation was totally gone. Instead she could feel the unmistakable crashing, flailing, and total disorientation that came with a major wipeout.

It was almost like her shark attack all over again—the one bad experience that haunted her so much, she still couldn't bear to surf in deep water. Only instead of a great white taking a chomp out of her board, it was her own daydreams getting munched in front of her.

Perfect. She'd had her first boyfriend for all of ten minutes and already she was stumped on what to do. There had to be something seriously wrong with her.

"Cass-*eeeeeeeee*!" A familiar female voice sang out her name.

Cassie turned and spotted her cousin Tori

bounding toward her as fast as her high-heeled wedge sandals would allow.

How does she do it? Cassie wondered. Somehow, Tori always seemed to be wearing a brand-new outfit. But how was that even possible since campers were only allowed one trunk? Did she have a secret closet in the jungle? Did she have a magic passageway to Barneys?

"Okay, so . . . ?" Tori planted herself right in front of Cassie and started making little circular motions with her right hand—with the perfect berry-polished manicure.

That was something else about Tori. In addition to her enormous invisible closet, the girl seemed to have discovered a salon somewhere among the banyan trees.

"What?" Cassie replied.

Tori made a huffing noise and put her hands on her hips. "So did he kiss you?"

"Yeah. I mean . . . no. Not really."

"What does *that* mean?"

"We were just about to when we had to stop."

Her cousin frowned. "But he was coming in for an actual kiss, right? He wasn't trying to whisper in your ear or something?"

Cassie thought for a moment. No, they had definitely been in pre-make out formation. His mouth had been heading for her mouth, not her ear. She knew what close whispering felt like and this was very different. This had been softer. Warmer. Tingly-er.

"It was a kiss. Or almost was, anyway."

Tori let out such a high-pitched squeal, Cassie fully expected a pack of dogs to come running up. "I'm so proud of you!" she gushed. She hooked her right arm around Cassie's left and started pulling her, half skipping, along the beach.

"Yeah, well. Don't congratulate me too soon," Cassie muttered. "Like I said, it wasn't technically a kiss."

"*Yet,*" Tori stressed, still smiling smugly.

"And he's in Waikiki for a couple of days."

"Big deal."

"With his ex-girlfriend."

Tori's grin vanished. "Okay. That's pretty bad. I'll give you that." Cassie sighed. She liked bubbly Tori better.

"But so what?" Tori asked. "He's had all this time to hook back up with Danica and he hasn't, right?"

"I guess not."

"That means it's really truly totally over. You know. Like when you can't even remember why you were into them in the first place."

"Uh, you forget, Tor. I've never had a boyfriend."

"Yeah, I know. But I meant guys you go out with."

"Had none of those either."

"Come on!" She bumped her shoulder against Cassie's. "You've had dates . . . right?"

Cassie shook her head.

"Seriously? Not even, like, a just-for-prom boyfriend?"

"Nada."

"But what about all those superhot surfer guys you travel with? You've at least started up something with one of them once upon a time? Right?"

Cassie shrugged. "I held hands with one or two while we walked on the beach."

Tori blinked back at her. "You held hands? That's it?"

"Why? What's wrong?"

"Nothing. That's . . . sweet. Really." Tori's smile

seemed to freeze in place until it looked more like a wince. "It's just . . . I always assumed you'd had at least one or two flings. I thought it was, like, one of the perks of your job."

"What are you talking about? That would be stupid. They're my teammates. It would be so . . . wrong. Like kissing family."

"So? I kissed Duncan at Aunt Alice's wedding. What's he? Like, our second cousin? Third cousin twice removed?"

"You are such a freak." Cassie smiled and shook her head. "If I started up something with one of my surf pals, it would seriously complicate things. Plus, I've never thought of any of those guys in that way."

They walked in silence for a moment. Suddenly Tori came to a dead halt and gasped.

"What?" Cassie instinctively searched the waves for shark fins.

"*Shhh!*" Tori pulled her behind a bush. "Over there. It's Eddie. He's with Larkin Fennell. Can you believe it?"

"Um . . . no." Cassie then took a moment to brace herself for the scorn of her cousin/social director. Then bravely she asked, "Who's Larkin Fennell?"

Like clockwork, Tori's jaw dropped. She stared at Cassie as if she were turning mint green before her eyes. "She's the snootiest camper in this place. Where have you been?"

Cassie looked over at the girl. She had brown eyes and long shiny brown hair. "She's pretty."

Tori made a snorting noise. "Best looks money can buy. Do you know she actually had a butler or something carry all her stuff to her bunkhouse? What a snot!"

Cassie frowned. "Why do you care who he hangs out with, anyway? He's your ex. I thought you were over Eddie."

Again her cousin stared at her in disbelief—with a little pity thrown in. "You don't get it, do you?"

"No. Explain it."

"It's complicated—the whole deal with exes. It's never totally over. You don't want them back, exactly. But you don't want them to be all happy and hooked up with someone else."

Cassie waited. "And this is *why*?" she prompted.

"Because. It just is."

"So *not* what I needed to hear right now,"

Cassie grumbled, thinking of Micah and Danica.

Tori's eyes widened in minor horror. "Oh, but no! That's not going to happen. Like I said, their relationship is completely finished."

"I hope so," Cassie mumbled, flicking a bug off her arm. "I really hope so."

A strawberry milkshake. No, chocolate with maraschino cherries—and extra whipped cream on top.

Danica fantasized about her favorite dessert while waiting for the slow-moving dude at baggage check to find her surfboard.

Back in Miami there was an old-fashioned diner just a couple of miles from her house. Danica and her friends used to bicycle over there and treat themselves. Of course, this was before they discovered that the beach was a much better place to meet guys—before they started worrying about fat and sugar intake. Seemed like she was happier then. In tense times Danica found herself craving those shakes and the sweet, cool, luscious comfort they'd given her.

She had to admit she was feeling a bit stressed out. She had thought she was over Micah, but it turned out she wasn't. Seeing Micah and Cassie about to kiss was a major blow. Plus, it didn't help that Micah spent the entire plane trip from the Big Island to Oahu staring out the window with a dopey smile on his face.

Did she ever make him space out like that when they were dating? She liked to think she had. But one thing she *did* know for sure was that it was never too late to try. And right now, she was determined to do just that.

"Got mine." Micah bounded up beside her with his board tucked under his right arm.

Danica let out a grunt. "Not me. I think the doofus decided to take a break in the middle of looking for my board."

"Aw, you know. They're busy," Micah said with a shrug. "I'm sure he'll get it as soon as he can."

Sometimes Micah's la-di-da attitude really got to Danica. But right then it didn't bother her at all. That's how she knew she was in deep. "You're probably right," she said, trying to match his sunny tone.

14

During the flight she had consoled herself with the fact that she had Micah all to herself these next couple of days. A lot could happen in that amount of time. And she hoped that by the end of the trip she would have wiped all traces of Cassie out of Micah's brain. So maybe on the flight back he'd be staring at *her* with big dopey eyes instead of the clouds.

She wasn't exactly sure how yet, but she'd do it.

A sudden roar of noise made them turn around.

"Great. Another plane is deboarding and they still haven't found my stuff," Danica grumbled, gesturing toward the pack of tanned, athletic-looking teens headed in their direction.

"Huh. I wonder if they're here for the competition, too."

Micah looked almost nervous. His Adam's apple kept appearing and disappearing as he swallowed repeatedly, and his left foot tapped out a hip-hop rhythm on the industrial carpeting.

The pack of surfers coming toward them did look pretty intimidating. They were tall and perfectly built, all decked out in top-of-the-line surfer wear. One in particular stood out. He had curly blond hair and droopy blue eyes and a swagger that told the world he was a hotshot. Plus he was cute in a drool-producing sort of way. He even looked somewhat familiar.

A couple of days ago Danica would have totally gotten her flirt on for this dude, but at that very moment, all she could think about was Micah.

"Okay, people. Let's get moving." Haydee seemed to suddenly appear, all laden down with bags and flipping through a half-dozen different papers. Behind her Zeke loped toward them, his head bobbing with every slow step. "No rental car because *somebody* forgot to make the reservation." Haydee turned to glare at Zeke, who didn't seem to notice.

Danica groaned. Haydee should have known better than to trust Zeke with such a task. The guy was only good at one thing—surfing—which was why he'd probably be Camp Ohana's male surf counselor until he went to the big sandy beach in the sky.

"All is not lost, however," Haydee went on. "Luckily I found a taxi that can take all of us and our stuff. But we've got to hurry. So come on, people! Danica, where's your surfboard?"

Just then the baggage claim attendant showed

up carrying her lucky board. "Here you go, miss," he said, handing it over.

Danica took it from him and ran her hands over it, checking for dings. Lucky for him it seemed to be in perfect condition. Otherwise the dude would've had to wear a broken surfboard on his head for the rest of the day.

"Good, good. Let's go now. We're on the meter." Haydee started charging through the crowds of people. Zeke, who had only just reached them, had to turn around and head back the way he came. Danica and Micah followed as best as they could with their boards in tow.

As soon as Danica stepped away from the baggage claim booth, the Surfer King and his posse walked up.

"Hey," he said, smiling and nodding at her as she passed.

Danica smiled back. Micah, she saw, noticed the exchange.

"You know that guy?" he asked as they headed out of the terminal area.

Ooh . . . he's jealous. That's a good sign, she thought to herself. "No. Why?"

He shrugged. "No reason. He just . . . looked familiar."

Haydee was now just a blond bob in the distance. But Zeke, who could only go fast when riding a wave, was right beside them.

"That was Bo Anderson, man," he said. "He won the Boost Mobile Pro last year."

"Aw, man! Right!" Micah suddenly looked worried. "Do you think he's here to compete?"

"At the Junior Surf Invitational?" Zeke made a face. "I don't think so. That dude's, like, sponsored by sports drinks and stuff. This thing is totally beneath him." He glanced worriedly at Micah and Danica. "No offense, guys."

"That's all right," Micah replied. Danica noticed he looked somewhat relieved, but his eyes were still darting around, checking out the fellow travelers.

"So . . . is your family gonna hop over and see you surf?" Zeke asked Micah. Danica could tell he was trying to change the subject after his stupid remark about the competition.

"Nah." Micah chuckled. "Just my luck they're on the mainland visiting relatives in St. Louis. I haven't even had a chance to tell them about this."

"Don't worry," she said, bumping him playfully with her shoulder since her hands were full. "Haydee's going to record the whole deal. You can upload it later on YouTube for all of them to watch."

"Hey, yeah. Thanks." He smiled at her and Danica sensed real honest-to-god warmth behind it.

Warmth. As in friendly. As in good ol' pal, chum, buddy Danica.

That's got to change, she thought as visions of frothy ice cream drinks danced through her mind.

"Guys! Come *on*!" Haydee was standing several yards in front of them, wildly waving her left arm.

As they trotted down the sloping ramp into the airport's main concourse, Danica felt a twinge in her left thigh. It was the cut she got while sitting on a broken wicker chair in Simona's office. Seemed like months ago she had sat in that torture device of a seat listening to the C.I.T. director gripe on and on about her behavior. And now look at her. Danica was here, on Oahu, representing the camp as their winning female surfer.

Things could sure change fast. And if her luck with Simona could reverse itself, so could the situation with Micah.

"Aloha! Welcome to Oahu." A beautiful woman with native features and a bright hibiscus-patterned dress stood greeting travelers. She leaned forward and placed a lei of purple orchids over Zeke's head.

"Mahalo," he said.

"And one for you." The lady turned and draped the same style lei over Micah.

"Thanks," he said, stepping aside so she could reach Danica.

"And for you—"

"Wait." Danica held up her free hand. "I want one of those," she said, gesturing to a pile of yellow leis on a nearby bench.

The woman looked confused.

Danica sighed. She knew they didn't have time for this. The guys were watching in bewilderment and Haydee was at the far end of the concourse shouting their names and signaling with her free arm as if trying to direct aircraft. But she didn't care. She was wearing a Kelly green top that would clash with the purple lei. And Haydee wanted to take pictures once they got to the hotel.

Everything had to be perfect.

"May I have a yellow one instead, please?" she asked sweetly.

"Of course." The lady's smile was starting to look forced. She set down the purple lei and snatched a yellow one from the nearby pile. "Welcome to Oahu," she said, placing the flowers over Danica's head. "I hope you enjoy your stay."

"Oh, I will," Danica replied. "I definitely will."

Micah stared out the window of the taxi van, watching the familiar terrain pass by. He'd made this drive from the airport dozens of times while visiting Oahu with his family. He knew every turn, every stop, every beach view. But this time it felt different. Everything seemed a little . . . unreal.

He still could barely believe he'd won Camp Ohana's surf expo. Sure, he'd worked hard and gave it his best shot, but he never actually let his mind go to that next step. He'd never imagined himself holding the trophy or getting congratulated. And he never ever saw himself getting flown to the Junior Surf Invitational.

If only Cassie had competed. She would have

won for sure and it would have been nice to have her there with him. Maybe they could have even finished the kiss they'd started earlier . . .

Micah slouched down in his seat and thought about Cassie. There was just something about her that made him feel as if sparks were shooting through him. Was it her looks? No. She was definitely gorgeous, but it was more than that. More than her sweet nature and sense of humor and awesome skills on the surfboard, too. Cassie just felt . . . right. He'd been drawn to her since that first day he saw her in that gold bathing suit. He could still see it in his mind . . .

Then again, maybe there was one tiny upside to Cassie not being there. If she was close by, he might be more focused on her than on the competition.

Micah suddenly realized that Haydee was talking to them.

". . . some traditional opening ceremony and buffet dinner . . ." she was saying. "Nothing fancy, but be on your best behavior anyway. Remember, you are representing Ohana. After dinner, we all go to bed early. It's been quite the day, and by sunset I'm sure we'll be wiped out."

Everyone looked at her.

"Sorry. I meant *tired*. Besides, we have a real early start tomorrow. The competition doesn't start till nine, but they want us down at the beach by seven thirty . . ."

It suddenly felt as if Micah's stomach had taken a hard right turn, even as the car continued straight ahead. Just the mention of "competition" caused his brain to seize up and made him unable to hear anything else.

That was something else that was strange about being here: He was nervous. He knew it was silly of him to be so shaky. After all, he'd been steady and focused at the camp expo.

But this competition was different. It was . . . more. More intense. More crowded. More everything. He just didn't want to let everyone down.

The seat shifted slightly as Danica yawned and stretched beside him. The next thing he knew, her head was resting on his right shoulder.

"Uh . . ." was all he could think to say.

"Man, I'm zonked," Danica murmured. She made a little birdlike noise and snuggled in closer, her right hand falling across his chest, her flower-scented hair right beneath his nose.

Micah looked up at Haydee, wondering if she would put a stop to it with a long lecture about PDA and representing Camp Ohana with proper modest behavior, but she was too busy leafing through a stack of forms. He then glanced over at Zeke, who was sitting on the other side of him, but the guy hadn't noticed it either. Instead he was staring out the window and mumbling something about the trade winds.

Micah sat straight as a longboard, wondering what to do. Should he make Danica stop? It wasn't that big a deal. It wasn't like they were kissing. Danica was probably just worn out from the trip and all the excitement, and the backseat *was* pretty crowded with the three of them. It didn't mean anything.

In fact, it was kind of . . . nice. After all, Danica was a friend. Sort of. He still cared about her even after the weirdness of their breakup. And the weirdness was pretty much gone now.

Besides, Micah was also tired. Gradually he relaxed again, easing back into a comfortable position. After a while, the regular swaying motion of the car and the sounds of the motor mixed with Zeke's steady mumbling made him drift off, too.

TWO

It worked.

Danica sat as still as she could, pretending to be napping. Micah, in the meantime, had actually fallen asleep. His head was resting against hers and his hand lay atop her forearm. She could smell that familiar Micah scent she had grown so accustomed to last summer: sunblock mixed with some sort of citrus-scented shampoo. It felt so cozy and comfy.

When she'd first cuddled up against him, she was halfway scared he'd ask her to stop—in his superpolite Micah way. But he didn't. Then he leaned into her all sweet and snug. It was just the proof she needed. Like, even though he acted as if he was totally over her, his body couldn't hide his true feelings.

The van slowed to a stop and Danica opened one eye halfway. They had pulled up at the Surfside

Hotel. A tiny wave of disappointment washed over her. Now she'd be back to dealing with in-denial Micah.

"Wake up, sleepyheads!" Haydee leaned forward and rapped on Danica's knee. "We've got checking in and unpacking to do."

"Huh?" Danica said, acting as if she were just now awakening.

Micah's head jerked up and he blinked, wondering where he was. Then he looked down at his hand resting on Danica's arm. Quickly he raised it over his head and pretended to stretch.

His eyes met hers and Danica could almost see the tension refilling.

She had to be careful of what she said. If she came on too strong, he'd avoid her as if she had the Ebola virus. But if she acted like nothing happened, that would be obvious, too.

"Uck!" she exclaimed, patting the top of her head. "I think you drooled in my hair."

That seemed to do it. Micah laughed and his shoulders returned to their normal elevation. "Sorry," he said. "Think of it as hair gel."

"Gross!" She gave him a playful shove.

The four of them spilled out of the van and hauled their luggage and equipment into the hotel lobby. Danica had been expecting someplace a little more upscale—with mood lighting and fountains and marble statues in the lobby. Instead she found herself in an older building, with maroon and navy patterned carpet right out of the 1990s, buzzy fluorescents, and lots of pale, elderly tourist ladies in muumuus.

If any of the others were disappointed in the digs, they weren't showing it.

"Thank god we're here," Haydee said, plopping her tweed duffel on the floor. "You guys are free to wander about while I check us in. But be back in ten minutes."

"*Yesss!*" Zeke raised his fist in the air. "Time to go pay homage."

"What are you talking about?" Danica found it strange that Zeke should be one of the adult chaperones considering he acted more like a kid than she did. "Pay homage to what?"

Zeke looked at her as if live shrimp were crawling out of her ears. "The Duke statue, man."

"The what?" she repeated, but Zeke was already loping out the front door.

Micah laughed. "Come on. I'll show you."

She followed the guys two blocks down to Waikiki Beach. The place was packed. Throngs of tourists with skin the color of marshmallow (soon to be carnation pink) littered the sandy shoreline. But even they couldn't spoil the view—the beautiful turquoise water glittering in the sunlight, and the familiar postcard image of Diamond Head looming up out of the water to their left.

Zeke led them down the sidewalk to a large bronze statue. It was of a man standing in front of a surfboard with his arms outspread.

"Duke Kahanamoku," Micah explained to Danica as Zeke, with reverence, placed his airport lei on one of the outstretched arms. "The Father of Surfing. He made the sport popular worldwide."

Danica stared into the dark metal face. He seemed like a nice guy. Most people would seem stuck-up with their arms out like that—all "Hey, look at me!" Instead he looked as if he were welcoming everyone to the beach.

Maybe someday they'd have a statue of her on the shores of Cocoa Beach, and visitors could leave *real* necklaces on her arms . . .

"Your turn," Zeke said, stepping down off the rock base of the monument.

Micah scrambled up and hung his lei on the opposite arm.

Danica suddenly didn't want to. It was her stupid lei. She'd gotten the right color and everything. Besides, she didn't want to bow down in front of this dude, no matter how nice he looked or how much he did for her sport. It would be like . . . handing over a piece of her power. "Nope. Not this time, guys," she said.

Micah just shrugged but Zeke looked at her as if she'd just pulled a gun on him. "What? You aren't gonna pay tribute?"

"We Florida surfers do our own thing."

"Okay." Zeke seemed to be backing away from her ever so slightly. "You want to snub the island, that's your business. But don't blame me if bad luck falls upon you."

"Whatever." Danica wanted to point out that if the statue was really so powerful, he probably wouldn't still be stuck working as Camp Ohana's laziest counselor. But she behaved. "What's that for?" she asked, changing the subject.

She pointed to a camera mounted on a nearby telephone pole.

"It's a webcam," Zeke explained.

"For security?"

"Well, yeah, maybe. But also so people can see you on the Internet."

"You mean people can see us right now? Online?" Danica absently smoothed her hair with her left hand.

"Yep. Oh, hey! That gives me an idea." Micah's face lit up so suddenly, it practically went *ding*. He pulled his cell phone out of his pocket, hit a couple of buttons, and pressed it against his ear.

"What's he doing?" Zeke asked.

"Probably calling his dad," Danica replied.

As she watched Micah pace around with his sleek red Nokia, muttering, "Come on, come on," a new thought pushed its way to the front of her brain.

"You still have my cell number programmed into your phone?" she asked him.

Micah's eyes lifted to hers. "Huh? Oh, yeah. It's in there. Why?"

"Just wondering," she said, staring out at the

ocean. "Thought it could be useful in case we get separated here."

It would be useful, but that wasn't why she asked about it. The fact that she was still one of his cell contacts was an excellent sign. It meant he hadn't fully deleted her from his life. It meant that he wanted her back in—even if he didn't realize it himself yet.

"Finally!" Micah exclaimed, doing an about-face. He pressed his phone against his right ear and covered his left ear with his hand. "Charlie? Hey, Charlie! It's Micah!"

Charlie! Disappointment crashed over Danica like an icy cold wave. *He was calling the camp office!*

"Yeah! We're in Oahu. In fact we're on Waikiki Beach right now! Hey, go get Cassie and bring her to the office. Don't ask, just do it! Get the whole gang!"

Danica clenched her fists reflexively. She hated hearing him shout Cassie's name. She knew it was just because he was on his cell at a noisy beach, but *still*. Broadcast your little obsession to the world, why don't you?

31

Micah spun back around and smiled at her and Zeke. "He's getting them."

Whoopee. Danica wondered if there was any way she could toss his phone into the surf and make it look like an accident.

"What? Yeah, I'm here!" Again Micah turned his back to her and shouted into the cell. "Who's there with you? Great! Now I want you to go to a website. Don't ask, just do it!"

Danica pretended to fiddle with the clasp of her bracelet as he hollered the URL to Charlie. Stupid phones. She had Micah all to herself for a change and what does he do? He calls camp. Maybe she should have put that lei on the dumb statue after all.

"Danica!" She glanced up to see Micah and Zeke in front of the camera. Micah was waving her over while Zeke kept striking different poses.

Fine. She'd play along. Danica sashayed over to the guys and stepped in between them. *"Cheese!"* she cried, throwing her arms around Micah.

Let Cassie watch. Let her see what she's missing out on.

He called. He asked for me. Charlie said he wanted me most of all.

Cassie kept turning these thoughts over and over in her mind like a lucky penny, hoping to take the edge off the burning sensation in her gut. There stood Micah, smiling and waving with one hand while holding his phone in the other. And there beside him—no, more like *on* him—was Danica, looking all perky and pretty and covered in flowers.

The sight of the Duke Kahanamoku statue—her favorite surfer of all time—barely even registered in her brain.

Thanks, Micah. It's sweet of you to want to say hi to me via the webcam, but I could do without the whole ex-girlfriend-clinging-to-your-side image.

"Can you see us?" came Micah's voice over the speaker phone.

"Yeah," everyone replied in unison. Besides her and Charlie, Tori, Andi, and Ben were all crammed into the tiny front room of the camp's main office.

"You guys are so lucky! I *love* Waikiki," Andi crooned. She bounced on the toes of her sneakers, causing her hair to spring about this way and that, like tiny explosions of reddish-brown curls. "Wish we could be there to cheer you on!"

"Me too," came Micah's reply. A second later they could see him mouth it via the website image.

Ben stooped over the phone receiver. "So you guys gonna kick some butt tomorrow or what?"

Then came a pause. Micah's shoulders hunched ever so slightly. "Yeah, I hope," he said, followed by a chuckle.

"Of course he is!" Tori said to Ben. Then she bent down over the phone. "You'll rule the place. This is Tori, by the way."

Another chuckle. Now Micah was shuffling his tennis shoes in the sand. "I figured it was you."

Cassie wished she could magically reach through the computer screen and throw her arms around Micah—the way Danica kept doing as she mugged for the webcam, only for different reasons. She wanted so badly to reassure him that he would do fine. That it was normal to be nervous before competition—terrifying thoughts of sharks notwithstanding.

Plus, she just wanted to be there, close to him, holding his hand and maybe even finishing up that kiss they started.

"Hey, um, guys? Could I talk to Cassie for a bit? I mean, like, alone. Not over speakerphone."

Cassie's mouth automatically boinged upward and her cheeks got all toasty. The others looked at her simultaneously, all wearing matching knowing grins.

"Sure thing," Andi said. "Good luck tomorrow, guys! Bye!"

One by one they filed out of the office, each of them casting smug glances at Cassie as they passed her. Charlie pushed a button on the phone and gave her the handset as he walked toward the door.

She peeked out the window and waited until they were safely out of earshot before placing the receiver to her ear.

"Hey," she said through her smile. For some reason, she just couldn't wipe the dopey-happy look off her face. Plus her knees were doing some sort of weird dance. Good thing he couldn't see her the way she could see him.

"Hi. How's it going?" he asked.

"Good."

"Good. So . . . what's been going on?"

"You know. Usual stuff." Cassie ransacked her

mind for something more to say—something clever and charming. "The fried potatoes were extra greasy this morning." She squeezed her eyes shut and groaned. Was that the best she could do?

He laughed. "Really? Sorry to hear it."

Silence. Cassie could hear the ticking of the office wall clock and the pounding of the surf several yards away. *Your turn, dingbat.* "So . . ." she began. She had wanted to tell him something. What was it? Oh yeah! "Hey, um . . . about tomorrow. You're going to be great."

"I hope so. That's nice of you to say."

"No, I mean it. I'm not just saying it to be nice. You know what to do. Just keep your head in it and forget about everything else. That's what I do." Oh, great. Now she sounded like a know-it-all.

"Thanks."

"Sure."

More silence. Was it her turn? Or his turn?

"I wish we could have had more time this morning," he said. "To, you know, finish some things."

Her dopey smile returned. "Me too."

A cozy second passed. Then another and

another. Soon it didn't feel cozy anymore. Once again that helpless, drowning sensation came over her. What was her problem? Why couldn't she think of anything to say?

"Um. Hey, Cass?" he said. "Sorry but . . . I've got to go."

"Oh . . . okay . . ." Cassie couldn't decide if she felt disappointed or relieved. Maybe both.

"Yeah. Haydee wants us back at the hotel. We need to unpack and get ready for some dinner thing."

"Okay. Well . . . have fun! Good luck tomorrow. You'll do great!" She winced at the tone of her voice. It came out all shaky and fake-sounding. Would he think she was lying?

"Thanks. I'll *mumble mumble mumble*." Cassie couldn't understand the last few words. On the computer monitor she could see him turn away from the camera and hunch over the phone. Then Haydee walked into view, talking and pointing behind her.

"I'm sorry, what?" Cassie asked, but at the same time he said, "Okay, gotta run. Bye!" and hung up. She could only watch as he followed Haydee offscreen.

What a dope. That conversation should have

made her day. If only she'd had a heads-up that he would call, she could have—what? Rehearsed some witty lines or flirty chit-chat, maybe. Or at least come up with a few direct questions. Instead she went all mute and boring. And when she did talk, she rambled out of control.

Now that she'd revealed how dorky she really was, he was probably rethinking his whole attraction to her. Someone like Micah probably preferred clever, confident girls—or at least girls who could talk.

Girls like Danica.

"There you are!" Tori ran toward her. "So? How'd it go?" She was still wearing that smirky little grin—the one all of the others had had on when they headed out of the office to give Cassie privacy.

"Okay, I guess."

Her cousin frowned. "What do you mean, 'I guess'?"

Cassie didn't want to go into it. She was too tired and confused. She was so looking forward to a quick dinner followed by bedtime. Maybe in the quiet of her bunkhouse she'd be able to organize her thoughts and figure some things out.

"We didn't have much time to talk," she explained. "Haydee showed up and made him get off."

"She is such a spaz," Tori said, shaking her head. Suddenly her eyes widened. She grabbed Cassie's left arm and yanked down. "Hey! Did you know that Charlie likes Andi?"

"Yeah, he told me," Cassie said.

"So why didn't you tell me?"

"I don't know. Because it was a secret. What's it to you, anyway?"

Tori's eyes sparkled in an unabashedly self-satisfied way. "Only that I'm the world's best matchmaker."

"Oh no. Tor, don't. Please?"

"Why not? The guy obviously needs help."

"Is that why he told you?" Cassie felt a rush of panic. Is that why he'd confessed his crush to her on that first day, when they were stuck in the closet during that game of truth or dare? Had he been hoping that Cassie would help him? If so, she'd totally let him down. Not that she would have been much help anyway.

"Um . . . yeah, sure. That's probably why he told me."

Cassie squinted at her cousin. Tori's voice was suddenly all breathy-sounding. A sure sign that she wasn't speaking the truth. "He didn't actually tell you, did he?"

"Okay, no. Not directly. But come on! It's *so* obvious! When we were all standing in the office, he couldn't take his eyes off of her. I can't believe I never noticed before."

"Do you actually think there's a chance for them? Do you think Andi feels the same way?"

Tori scrunched up her nose. "I don't know . . . I'd have to say no, she doesn't. Not at the moment. But I don't think she's all hung up on anyone else either—at least from what I've seen."

"How can you even tell? The girl's always on the go. I'm not even sure what color her eyes are."

"I know, but I really think she could get into Charlie. We just need to get them alone together. After all, he is cute. In a teacher's pet sort of way."

"Yeah. He is." She had to admit Charlie had a goofball charm about him. "You sure it's that simple, though?"

"Of course. Boy plus girl plus time always equals those kinds of thoughts. She won't be able to help it."

Didn't need to hear that, Cassie grumbled inwardly. She thought of Danica hanging on Micah, and all the together time they were having on Waikiki.

"Talking is the best way to get a romance going," Tori continued. "That's what Oprah says. Or maybe it was Dr. Phil. Or maybe it was that blond girl on *The Hills*. I can't remember."

"I see," Cassie said—even though she didn't.

"So that's it then. We'll help Charlie."

We? Cassie wondered. Since when was she considered an expert? She couldn't even talk on the phone right.

"Cassie? Hey, Cassie!"

Cassie spun around at the sound of her name. Simona, the head counselor, was running toward her, all pink-faced and puffing.

"I've been looking everywhere for you. Then Charlie told me you were in the office. You must have shown up right after I left," she said, gasping for breath after every fourth word. She glanced over at Tori and frowned. "Young lady, shouldn't you be with your group?"

"I was just . . ."

"I'm tired of hearing from your counselor about your inability to follow the schedule. This is a camp, not a resort, Victoria. You can't just come and go as you please."

Faint lines appeared on Tori's forehead and her bottom lip slid up to cover her top one. Cassie couldn't tell if she was upset by Simona's scolding or the fact that she'd been called "Victoria."

Gradually Tori's expression crumbled. "Yes, ma'am," she said somewhat meekly, staring down at her feet.

"Good." Simona gave a satisfied nod. "Now get to where you're supposed to be. I need to talk with Cassie."

"Fine!" Tori muttered, then stalked off down a nearby path.

"What's up?" Cassie asked Simona, once Tori was out of earshot.

"I just wanted to make sure you knew to report to the beach extra early tomorrow."

"Uh . . . sure . . . can I ask why?"

Simona scowled. "Didn't Haydee tell you? I knew it!" She let out an annoyed sigh. "I suppose she was just too busy to let you know that you're going to fill in as official surf C.I.T. while Danica and Micah are away."

"Oh. Uh . . . okay."

"I really appreciate it, Cassie. You're a lifesaver," Simona said, patting her shoulder. "I know you'll do a bang-up job!"

Cassie did her best to smile back. She really hoped the words *lifesaver* and *bang-up* weren't meant literally. Now not only was she worried about Micah, her head was filling with horrible images of chomping sea creatures and riptides and beginning surfers getting swept out to sea . . .

So much for her relaxing evening.

Chicken adobo . . . fish kebabs . . . *lomi-lomi* . . . homemade macaroni and cheese . . . a three-tiered rack of desserts . . .

Micah scanned the buffet table. Dozens of his favorite dishes all in one place. He would dive right in—if only his midsection didn't feel like it was being shoved through a cheese grater.

As he stood in the buffet line, trying to decide what his stomach would and wouldn't object to (so far rice and a biscuit were the only contenders), he noticed a shaggy-topped shadow looming over him. Looking back, he saw Bo Anderson, that swaggery surfer dude he'd noticed at the airport.

Bo noticed Micah staring and nodded at him. "'Sup?" he said with a grin. "Anything good here?"

"Probably. But I'll never know. Just . . . can't eat."

Bo nodded again, this time faster. "You competing in the morning? Man, I'm the same way. Won't eat much before and then pig out afterward. If these guys were smart, they would have planned this big thing for *after* the contest."

Micah laughed. He liked this guy, although he also sort of made Micah feel kind of nervous.

The dude's head continued to bob up and down, his blond curls following a half-second behind. "Yeah, hardly any of us eat the night before. This guy I practice with, Jonah, he always can—but he's more animal than human. This girl Cassie sure can.

44

We even call her Hot Dog because this one time—"

"Wait a minute," Micah interrupted. "You're not talking about Cassie Hamilton, are you?"

"Yeah! Heard of her, huh? You a fan?"

Micah felt a huge surge of annoyance. "Um, no. I mean, yeah, but . . . I know her, actually." He wasn't sure how else to put it. He was her friend? No, more than that. Her boyfriend? Pretty sure, but considering they'd only near-kissed it seemed technically wrong to call himself that. Her wannabe main dude? That was pretty accurate, but also extremely lame-sounding.

Bo's eyes grew almost as big as the plate in his hands. "What a weird coincidence, man. Cassie and I are supertight."

"Really?" Micah's gut felt like it was being skewered by hundreds of toothpicks. "That is weird."

The guy held out one of his palms. "I'm Bo, by the way."

"Micah." He gripped Bo's hand and gave it a firm shake.

"Micah . . . Micah . . . huh. I don't remember her talking about a Micah."

Another wave of irritation swept through Micah.

"Yeah, well . . . we just met a few weeks ago. She's at my camp this summer. Camp Ohana. I'm representing them in the contest tomorrow." He hoped the last bit would make him seem a little cooler in Bo's eyes.

Instead Bo's head shook in a cartoonish double-take. "She . . .what? She's at a camp? Whoa! I knew she was taking some time off, but what the heck is she doing in a place like that?"

Micah took a deep breath. He was past the geek-out phase. Great or not, he was *this close* to shoving the guy's whiskered face into the mac 'n' cheese. "She's one of the counselors-in-training. So am I," he explained. Then, unable to help himself, he added, "Guess you haven't talked to her in a while, huh?"

"Nah. Been on tour and stuff. I really should call her though. Cassie's great. Isn't she?"

He smiled and Micah could see no trace of smugness. *Maybe the guy isn't a jerk*, he decided. *Maybe he's just clueless.*

And yet he couldn't help wondering how "supertight" Bo and Cassie had been—or maybe still were.

"Yeah. She's great."

Bo glanced about as if he'd only just realized where he was. "Well, guess I better grab some more food before it's gone. Nice to meet you."

"Nice to meet you, too."

Bo started to walk off, then stopped and turned back toward Micah. "Oh, and hey. Good luck tomorrow. Take it from a pro: Having no appetite is a good thing. Means your whole body is focused on the competition." He clapped Micah on the back. "Being really nervous is totally cool."

"Thanks."

As Bo loped off toward the dessert cart, Micah fought the urge to throw a biscuit at his head. Who'd that guy think he was? *Take it from a pro?* Talking about how Micah must be *really nervous?*

Was the dude trying to make him feel better? Or make him explode from pent-up stress?

And, most importantly, *how well did he know Cassie?*

"I see you're on the high-carb diet."

Micah had been so busy frowning at Bo's back that he didn't notice Danica walk up beside him. He turned and directed the frown at her. "So what if I am?" he asked.

"Just kidding!" Danica squealed. "Jeez. Did that guy get to you or something?"

"Yeah. No. I don't know." Micah let out a sigh. "He was just trying to be nice . . . I think."

"You know you're not going to be competing against him, right?"

Micah still had images of Bo and Cassie in his mind, so it took him a moment to realize Danica was talking about tomorrow's surf contest. "I'm not?"

"No. He and a few others are only here for a special exhibition."

"How do you know this?"

"Because he's on the posters!" she said, laughing. She pointed to a nearby wall where a giant full-color flyer advertising the surf competition was displayed. A square filled with Bo's shaggy head was superimposed over a shot of the beach.

"Oh." Micah felt a little silly, but no less panicked.

"Hey." Danica stepped in close and playfully tapped the tip of his nose with her index finger. "Mellow out."

"Yeah, yeah."

"I mean it. You worked hard to get here. Loosen up and enjoy it a little more."

Micah could feel a smile work its way across his mouth. She was right. It was stupid of him to get freaked like this. He was supposed to be having fun.

"Thanks," he murmured. "I needed that."

"What can I say? I'm just awesome that way." Danica lifted her chin in a haughty angle and continued on to their table.

He shook his head and laughed. Maybe things weren't so bad after all. Bo might not be the jerk Micah supposed him to be. And although he still wished Cassie could be here, at least he had Danica. There was something comforting about having her around—in some ways she still knew him better than anyone else. Of course he hoped that someday Cassie would be the one who knew him best. If only he knew how close she and Bo had been—and maybe still were. Maybe then he could relax.

Danica checked her reflection in the mirrored wall of the elevator and grinned. Her green-blue eyes shimmered like flames on a gas stove and her mouth was curled in a tiny Mona Lisa–style grin. She knew that look—her can't-be-beat expression. She only wore it in the summer at Camp Ohana.

Progress was made today. Micah actually loosened up a bit. He still seemed distracted, but he shot her a few smiles over dinner (not that he ate much) and laughed at a couple of things she said. With just a little more quality one-on-one time, she could probably wipe what's-her-name out of his mind.

At this point Danica needed to focus on winning the competition. Then, by lunchtime tomorrow, she could turn her whole attention to Micah. Just a few more charged moments and things would be back to normal—back to where they were supposed to be. She'd be Micah's favorite, not Cassie. She'd be the triumphant surfer and star of the camp, not Cassie. Danica would once again be the awesomest one of all.

She was so close. All she needed was a relaxing bath and a good night's sleep and she'd be at the top of her game. Thank god Haydee let her beg out of listening to the boring welcome speeches so she could head back to the room and get ready for tomorrow.

Danica let out an impatient huff as the elevator stopped at the second floor lobby. The doors opened and four tall, athletic-looking girls stepped inside. They each smiled at her—tight, phony smiles that were just excuses to size her up.

They were obviously fellow surf competitors. In fact, Danica recognized them from the welcome dinner. They had been sitting at the back of the ballroom. Probably snuck out the door and up the stairs to the lobby before anyone noticed. Slick move.

"Hi," said the steeliest-looking one of the four, a ridiculously muscular girl with short black hair. "You here for the contest?"

"Mm-hm." Danica pretended to be barely interested in them.

"Supposed to have some major waves tomorrow. Hope you brought your game."

Danica looked the girl straight in the eye. "Oh, I can handle it. I'm ready for anything."

The girl smiled and held her stare. Danica was thrilled when she finally blinked and looked down.

"Ooh!" the girl gasped. "Look at your leg! How did you do that? Bad wipeout?"

"No!" Danica was suddenly acutely aware of the scab on her thigh. "I didn't wipe out. It's nothing. No big deal."

"Must itch like crazy, huh?"

"No," Danica lied. It did itch. A lot, now that she mentioned it. She must have sounded unconvincing because the other girls began murmuring among themselves.

The lead girl made a few *tsk-tsk* noises with her tongue. "Man, any weakness, even something small like that, can totally throw you off your game. Cuts always take forever to heal when you keep getting into salt water. And it's so tough to keep the sand out of them, isn't it?"

Danica considered not responding, but that would give the girl too much satisfaction. People like this needed to be dealt with directly, mind game versus mind game. Something Micah, who was too nice for his own good, really needed to learn.

She met the girl's gaze and held it. "Don't stress yourself. It is so not a problem. I can't even feel it."

Danica kept on grinning at the girl as if she were her long-lost best friend. She held her stare, watching the girl's expression go from smug to doubtful to simply annoyed. Finally the elevator dinged to a stop and the doors slid apart.

"Here I am," Danica sang out cheerfully as she pranced out into the corridor. "So nice to meet you. Good luck tomorrow!"

"You too," said the tough girl as her pals stood and smirked behind her. "And take care of that leg. It looks pretty bad."

Before Danica could respond, the doors closed between them. She stood there, fuming—hoping to hear a loud snapping sound and the screams of four snooty girls as the elevator plummeted several stories.

Forget them, she told herself. *She was just trying to rattle you. And it didn't work.*

She spun around and headed for her room, her left hand reaching behind to scratch the scab on her thigh.

Three

"Danica? Danica! It's almost 6 A.M. Wake up!"

Underneath the ugly palm-leaf-patterned bedspread, Danica's hands formed into fists. What Haydee didn't realize was that Danica *was* awake. She had been since 4 A.M. She just didn't feel like getting up yet. Or opening her eyes.

All night long Danica tossed and turned, trying to forget about the scab on the back of her leg. But the more she tried to forget about it, the more she thought about it and the more it itched.

Was it her imagination, or was it getting worse? What began as an occasional annoying tingle was now a constant throb. Maybe while she slept (or didn't sleep) she'd developed a rare fatal infection. It even seemed a little puffier when she touched it.

"Danica!"

Haydee's normal tone of voice was practically a shout, so that when she actually did yell, it almost shattered windows.

"Okay, okay," Danica mumbled, pushing herself into a sitting position. She'd only been trying to get some extra rest since her night went so badly. Plus, she knew exactly how long it took to get herself ready. She still had time.

"You've got to get a move on if you want some sort of breakfast," Haydee said as she bustled about the room, repacking a few things and snatching her cell phone off the charger. Danica noticed she had actually remade her double bed.

Who makes their bed in a hotel? she wondered. Even a cruddy hotel had maid service for that sort of thing.

Her thigh ached as she slid out of bed. It felt as if some gnawing, sharp-toothed creature had ahold of it. She needed to do something about it before she went completely bonkers.

In one sudden, dizzying movement, Danica grabbed her makeup case and headed for the bathroom.

"Don't take too long in there," Haydee called

out. Danica replied by locking the door with a loud *click*.

Medicine . . . bandages . . . topical creams . . . thank god her parents had tossed this stuff into her trunk before she left for camp. For the first time in her life she was glad her mom was kind of paranoid and controlling. Danica took out the assortment of tubes and boxes and scanned the labels for any mention of "numbing" or "itch relief."

Bang, bang, bang! Haydee's knocks were about as subtle as her voice.

"Hey in there," she called through the door. "Don't spend all day primping. We've got to be at the beach in forty-five minutes!"

Yeah, yeah. Do some deep breathing before you pop a blood vessel.

After washing her wound, applying ointments, and putting on a large, square-shaped bandage, Danica felt a little better. Now she didn't have to worry about it while surfing.

Bang, bang! "Danica! Open up!"

"Hang *on*." Danica studied her handiwork one last time and then tossed the first-aid supplies back into her bag. But she didn't open the door.

Because *now* it was time to primp.

Cassie pushed her scrambled eggs to the left side of her plate and frowned at them. They sure looked extra gooey today. She then scraped them over to the right side, next to her toast, but they didn't look any better over there. Even the toast appeared stale and unfit for human consumption—like a square piece of cardboard.

She knew she should eat something, but she was just too nervous about being the one and only surfing C.I.T. that day.

It was strange. She'd always been able to eat before competitions—even major ones. Now all she had to do was teach some kids the basics of surfing and she couldn't even face her breakfast.

But this was different. It wasn't fear of losing a contest . . . it was fear of losing a limb. Or—even worse—freezing up with terror and being too useless to prevent a poor kid from drowning or becoming a shark's lunch or getting carried to Australia on a rogue wave.

She pushed away her plate and rested her head in her hands. Maybe she should just confess everything to Simona.

"Uh-oh."

Cassie glanced up to see Andi staring at her warily. "What? What is it?"

"You aren't eating," Andi said, nodding at Cassie's plate.

"Yeah. I'm . . . I'm just not that hungry today." She really hoped Andi wouldn't ask her *why* she had no appetite.

"Do you feel okay?" Andi leaned across the picnic table and placed her hand on Cassie's forehead. "How's your stomach?"

"Um . . . it's . . . well . . . it's feeling weird, actually." Cassie was telling the truth, but she still felt dishonest. Instead of meeting Andi's gaze, she glanced past her at Charlie, who was sitting at the next table over, staring dreamily at Andi's back.

Andi shook her head in a pitying way. "I bet you've got it."

"Got what?"

"Didn't you hear? Ben's got some awful virus thing. He was in the infirmary with a high fever last

58

night. Now he's back in his bunk and won't eat. The guys say he just lies there in a ball moaning. Can you believe it? Big, tough Ben?"

"No. He must feel awful."

"Girl, I hate to tell you this, but I think maybe you've got it." Andi leaned away from her dramatically, and once again Cassie noticed Charlie looking in their direction, all moony-eyed.

Cassie opened her mouth to disagree. After all, she wasn't running a fever and she'd barely gotten within two feet of Ben in a couple of days. It was definitely just nerves. But then she had another thought: Why not go with it? She was sorry to hear about Ben's puking and all, but this could actually be a good thing—at least for her.

"Yeah, I really haven't been feeling that great," she said, making her face go slack.

"You should go lie down."

"Can't." Cassie shook her head. "Gotta be surf C.I.T. today."

"Better go tell Simona you can't. This is no time to be brave."

The word *brave* made Cassie's gut do a somersault. If only Andi knew the truth.

"Well, no offense, but . . . I'm going to wash my hands." Andi got to her feet, held her palms out in front of her and started backing away from Cassie as if she were waving a semiautomatic weapon. "Hope you feel better!" With a flounce of curls, she headed out the door of the mess hall into the bright sunshine beyond.

Charlie looked so disappointed, Cassie felt like walking over and patting the top of his head.

Now for the tough part. She slowly rose to her feet and took her tray to the wash window. She dumped her food into the trash can—and walked over to Simona's table.

The C.I.T. director was bent over a bowl of crunchy cereal. Her right hand grasped the spoon and her left hand held a small stack of official-looking papers. She was so busy chomping and looking over the documents, she didn't notice Cassie standing right beside her.

"Um . . . excuse me?" Cassie reached out and tapped her on the shoulder.

"What is it?" Simona's head jerked around so quickly that Cassie backed up a step.

"S-sorry to interrupt. But . . . I'm not feeling well . . . and Andi told me about Ben and . . ."

"Is it your stomach?" Simona frowned at Cassie's midsection.

"Yes. I can't eat and . . ."

"Great." Simona let out a frustrated groan. "I knew this would happen."

"I'm sorry."

"No. It's not your fault." She looked back up at Cassie and smiled, but the stress still showed on her face. "It just seems like this happens every summer: Things go wrong all at once. Here I'm down two counselors and two C.I.T.s because of the surf invitational and we get hit by a stomach virus." She sighed heavily. "Guess we'll cancel surf lessons until you're better or the others come back—whatever comes first."

"Sorry," Cassie said again. She felt horrible about letting her down, especially since she wasn't really sick. But she was also immensely relieved. Her mental images of novice surfers getting swept out to sea faded away . . .

"Stop apologizing." Simona's spoon hand gave a little wave as if pushing away Cassie's words.

"You can't help it. I'd send you to the infirmary, but there's nothing they can do for you. Go back to your bunk, and please make sure everyone stays away from you! We don't need any more C.I.T.s down with this."

Cassie nodded. "Got it. Thanks." She turned and trudged out of the mess hall, feeling much better than she had when she went in.

No sooner had she gone a few steps along the gravel path then Tori came bounding up and fell into step beside her.

"Hey! Guess what!"

Cassie glanced all around them. "*Shhh!* Don't let Simona see you talking to me. I'm sick and supposed to keep away from everyone. Besides, you're supposed to stay with your group. Remember?"

Tori ignored her last comment. "You're sick?" she asked, glancing her up and down. "You don't look sick."

"I've got a stomach thing." Cassie winced at the whiny tone in her voice. She never was a good liar. "I couldn't eat breakfast at all." There. At least that was true.

"Yuck. Sorry. So whatcha gonna do all day?"

Cassie shrugged. "I don't know. Sleep. Hide out. Get better."

"You know what you need? You need me to care for you."

"But you're not supposed to wander around."

"It's not like I'm going to dive off a cliff, I'm walking with a counselor-in-training. A responsible *older* person." She grinned mischievously.

Cassie wasn't sure how to argue with that. At this point they had reached the C.I.T. bunkhouse. Tori stepped in front of her and raced up the steps. When she got to the top, she paused to look down at Cassie. "Come on, sickie!"

Cassie could only shake her head and tramp up the stairs after her. Leave it to her cousin to turn Cassie's "illness" into a social event.

By the time she stepped into the bunkhouse, Tori was already moving about the room, stirring up bedcovers and other belongings like a pint-size hurricane.

"Here you go," she said, patting Cassie's cot. "Make yourself comfortable. I'll put the iPod here. We'll just listen to the mellow song list instead of the dance one. And here are the latest issues of *Justine* and *Cosmo*. Oh, and I can run and get you some ginger ale. That's what Mom always gets me when my stomach hurts. Only . . . I don't know if they have any here. Probably just lemonade."

"What are you doing?" Cassie asked, staring at her in astonishment.

Tori paused long enough to shoot her an incredulous look. "What do you mean? I'm trying to cheer you up while you're sick."

"But . . . you can't just make yourself at home. You have stuff to do. You haven't even eaten yet."

"Sure I have. I brought a huge box of yogurt bars in my luggage. I hate the stuff they make here. No wonder you're sick." She pulled a bottle of nail polish out of her bag, sat down on a nearby chair, and started unscrewing the top. "Besides, it's still free time. Morning sessions don't start for a while."

Cassie glanced from the iPod to the magazines to the bottle of peach-colored liquid Tori was currently brushing onto her toes. "I can't believe you carry all this stuff around with you."

Tori shrugged. "Have you ever seen me bored?"

Cassie had to admit she hadn't. She let out a

yawn and flopped down on her bed. Even though she wasn't sick, she suddenly felt tired.

"Oh! Oh, oh! I still haven't told you!" Tori stopped in the middle of her big toenail and glanced up at Cassie, her eyes so big, they covered half her face.

"What?" Cassie perked up, pushing herself onto her elbows.

"Eddie isn't with that Larkin girl after all! In fact, I heard he doesn't even like her all that much. Isn't that great?" She bounced around on the seat of the chair in a small sort of victory dance.

Cassie shook her head. "It's so wrong that this makes you happy. You don't even want the guy anymore."

"Cassie, Cassie, Cassie. When will you understand? It's not about him. It's about me. It's about me not being replaced so fast and easy. Means I'm still awesome."

"Whatever." Cassie collapsed back down onto her back and stared at the wooden planks of the ceiling. There was obviously a lot she still had to learn about relationships. In a way, it seemed harder than calculus. It definitely made less sense.

"Knock, knock," someone sang out from beyond the screen door. It creaked open and Alexis, the swimming counselor, stepped into the room. "Hey," she said shooting Cassie a sympathetic look. "I heard you're sick with that stomach thing."

"Yeah." Cassie tried her best to look pitiful.

"Sorry to hear it. I just stopped by to see if you needed anything."

"That's nice. But I'm okay. Tori's taking care of me right now."

Tori waved "hello" with the nail brush.

"You really should get down to the beach, Tori," Alexis said. "You know you have a swim lesson in ten minutes."

"Aw, not today. Cassie needs me."

"Cassie can take care of herself. And you're already on Simona's gripe list for blowing off activities," Alexis countered. "Besides, Cassie will rest better alone. In *quiet*."

Tori flashed her an insulted expression. "Fine. If you think swimming is more important than my favorite cousin, then so be it." She put the top on her polish and dropped it into her still-bulging hobo bag.

What else could she possibly have in that thing? Cassie wondered.

"Feel better," Alexis said to Cassie before disappearing from the doorway.

"I'll try and stop by later to check on you," Tori said in a low voice. "Take it easy!" Then she, too, headed out the squeaky screen door.

The sounds of their footsteps tromping down the stairs grew fainter and finally stopped altogether. Cassie lay on her bunk and listened. There were no sounds, just the barest shushing noise of the ocean in the distance and an occasional peep from a bird. Otherwise the silence was strong—harsh, even.

Liar, the quiet seemed to say. *Phony.*

It was right. She was a big fat faker. She was actually pretending to be sick to get out of surfing— not even that, to get out of *teaching* surfing.

She'd never stooped so low in her life.

There it was. That's the one he wanted. The one he needed.

And it was the final heat.

67

Micah had already caught three waves and needed his required fourth. And if he wanted to place, this one seriously mattered. His first runs were okay. He'd managed to tweak out some moves and rack up points, but a couple of his maneuvers hadn't worked out. He still wasn't good in the tight spots. The best he could hope for was a stellar ride without too much jostling for position.

He had surfed this beach countless times before, so he knew he could take the time to wait for his ideal waves. He was confident they'd come. And he knew how to line up his marker on the beach—in this case, the one corner of the pink stucco Royal Hawaiian hotel—so that he'd be right in their path.

He could tell this was his wave by the way it rose, all fat and clean. And he was nearest to the peak. It was there just for him. Not only that, but it was the perfect day. Great weather. Light offshore winds. He had no excuses.

Micah waited until he felt the wave lift him high, then he jumped onto his board and took off with it.

Yes! This was his wave all right. He loved that feeling when everything became one—one force, one entity. When he didn't even have to work that hard at balancing and could let himself get carried along atop his watery platform—as if he were riding on a parade float.

Seconds later, the wave broke and shot him right into its center. There he was, in the middle of a liquid world, streaking along like he belonged. He forgot the stands and the judges' table. He forgot the incredible exhibition runs that Bo and others had done for the crowd right before the competition. He simply lost himself in the rush.

He even managed a nice cutback before the ride ended. Nothing too showy. And it wasn't the smoothest one ever made. But the conditions were perfect, so why not?

All too soon it was over. Micah was stepping out of the water, carrying his board and trying not to look at the scoring platform. *Let it be a surprise*, he told himself. *Nothing I can do about it now.*

He thought he would feel relieved, but instead he was kind of sad it was over. Truth was, he had enjoyed himself out there. He'd stopped thinking about the competition and just focused on the wave.

It was like one of those Zen-like sayings

Zeke was always muttering. He became "one with the water."

"Man, nice ride."

Micah glanced over to see a figure silhouetted against the sun. He recognized the shaggy hairdo immediately. "Hey, Bo," he greeted. "Thanks. Thanks a lot."

"Seriously, that was awesome. You have real style."

"Yeah, well . . . it's not like I did aerials or anything." Micah felt self-conscious taking a compliment from someone like Bo.

"No, dude. I mean it. Style is something you can't learn—you're born with it. And hey. You gotta be able to rip the small waves!" He slapped Micah on the back and almost sent him stumbling forward into the surf.

"Thanks," Micah said again, correcting his balance. "You were pretty awesome in the exhibition runs."

"I do it for the free luau food," he said with a shrug and lopsided smile. "So why isn't Cassie here?"

"She didn't compete."

"Probably not allowed to because of her pro

status, huh? I guess that's fair. But why isn't she here cheering you guys on?"

"Oh, well . . . you know. They could only send the four of us. Besides, Cassie's back at camp working. Probably giving lessons right this minute."

"Man . . ." Bo shook his head. "I still can't believe she's doing that. What a waste. That girl is so hot out on the water."

Micah didn't say anything. Instead he glanced down the beach where the female competitors were all stretching and getting ready for their runs. He could see Danica checking over her board, looking as confident as ever.

"But don't get me wrong," Bo went on. "It's cool, too. Noble, sort of. So . . . she teach you any moves?"

"Huh?"

"On the surfboard. She teach you any of her trademark stuff?"

"Uh . . . no."

"Aw, too bad. She's awesome." Bo looked out at the waves and chuckled. "Yeah," he added in a faraway-sounding voice, "she and I have had a lot of fun together. Cassie's definitely my girl."

Micah frowned at Bo's wide, tanned back.

Exactly what kind of "fun" was he talking about? What did he mean she was *his girl*?

"So . . . what did you say this camp was called?"

"Ohana." Micah managed to keep a growl sound out of his voice. "Camp Ohana. On the Big Island."

"Ohana," Bo repeated. "Huh. Maybe I'll send her a postcard or something. Anyhow, it's good to know she has some pals she can hang with while she takes this little break." He reached over and mussed the back of Micah's wet hair. "See you around," he said, and then loped away toward the roped-off VIP section of the beach.

Micah absently touched the back of his skull. He couldn't help feeling like a dweeby kid palling around with the older, cooler boys. What did Bo think? That he was some little newbie?

Even worse . . . was that how *Cassie* saw him?

Four

I'm it.

Danica kept saying it over and over in her head. *I'm it.* It was short and sweet and to the point. Just two syllables that summed up her mind-set.

She had to keep thinking it so that she couldn't let in any other thoughts. Nothing was going to distract her and keep her from winning this competition.

Of course the second she hit the beach she saw Elevator Girl and her posse. They flashed her fake smiles and a couple of them even waved. She didn't give them the satisfaction of playing along. Instead she kept her eyes focused straight ahead and walked to the check-in table as if she had all day.

Amateurs, she told herself. *They have no idea who they're dealing with.*

Maybe back home they could rattle her. Back

in Florida where everyone knew everything about her and her family—but not here. Here she ruled. For years she had perfected her image. She no longer had to pretend to be confident and accomplished; she really was all those things. And no one could take it all away.

"You're in the first group," Haydee said, jogging up next to her. "That's okay, right?"

"That's awesome, actually. I love being first." It was true. That way she didn't have to wait. She could go out there and show everyone her stuff and set the bar for the other competitors. People usually remember whoever went first and she liked that. Those that followed behind usually stayed that way: behind.

I'm it . . . I'm it . . . I'm it . . .

She kept it going throughout the boys' competition, pretending to watch them while she instead focused on the horizon and kept up her mental chant. She couldn't let anything else into her head—not even Micah. There would be time for that later. *After* she won.

"Yes! Yes! He looked great, didn't he?" Haydee exclaimed, shaking Danica by the shoulders.

"Yeah," Danica lied. No way was she going to confess that she was actually watching a ship in the distance.

"They're so slow with the scoring today," Haydee went on. "Hopefully they'll have results before you paddle out, but I don't think so."

"Oh well." *Stop talking to me.* Haydee's voice kept interfering with the voice in her mind.

"That's it! They just called for your heat. Go! Go kick some butt!"

I'm it . . . I'm it . . . I'm it. Danica's chant kept rhythm with her footsteps as she crossed the beach and waded into the water. She bellied onto her board and paddled into the waves, glad to finally be able to move about.

Something—she wasn't sure what—made her turn her head and glance to her left. She felt a bit like Spider-Man, the way he tingles whenever evil comes near. Or maybe her neck just needed to stretch that direction. Whatever the reason, she wished she hadn't. Because now she was staring right into the smug face of Elevator Girl as she swam out beside her.

"Hey there. How's the leg?" she said.

Danica faced out to sea again, but it was too late. Suddenly she was keenly aware of the scab on her thigh. It even twinged in response. And she'd been doing such a good job of focusing!

I'm it . . . she restarted. *I'm it . . . I'm it . . .*

But somehow it sounded different inside her head. Her inner voice seemed way less sure of herself.

She just had to concentrate and do what she came to do.

There. Rising in the near distance was a beautiful wave. Nice and clean, dark with depth. And she was closest to its peak. It was all hers!

Danica got into position, felt the wave pick her up, and immediately stood up tall. She loved this part best—that top-of-the-world feeling when you're atop a cresting wave. Together, the board and the water picked up speed, and Danica balanced herself perfectly, enjoying the wind on her face and the rush of power beneath her feet.

Now all she had to do was ride it. She could see the judges' stand and the bleachers full of spectators. All eyes were on her.

Concentrate, she told herself. *You know what*

you're doing. Just stay focused and don't think about the scratch . . .

"Oh no."

The second the word *scratch* entered her mind, Danica's left leg bobbled ever so slightly—as if the wound itself was moving it. She felt her balance shift to the right. She tried to counter by leaning left, but she went too far and had to tilt right again. Panic shot through her like ice water. Her whole body tensed and her board began to waver.

She had time for one last thought: *No!* Then she fell sideways into the surf.

There was darkness and bubbles and a loud rush of noise. Grit from the wave coursed over her skin. Her mouth filled with salt water. Danica felt the leash jerk against her leg as her surfboard shot the opposite direction. And then, finally, she resurfaced.

She took a loud gasping breath and pushed her hair out of her face. She had just caught a quick glimpse of the beach when another wave pounded her. This one pushed her forward several yards to where her feet touched bottom.

Feeling numb, she tugged her board to her, undid the strap, and slowly waded back onto shore.

Her ears were still full of water so she couldn't make out what the announcer said, but she heard his amplified voice burble something, followed by slight applause. Soon she was stepping out of the surf and onto dry beach. Her legs were shaking. Her eyes stung. Noises were muffled and strange. Only her heartbeat twanged loud and clear.

And people were staring. Everywhere she turned there was someone looking at her with round, pity-filled eyes.

"Stop it," she murmured to no one in particular.

Her right ear cleared just in time for her to hear Haydee shout her name.

"Are you okay?" she cried, running up to Danica and stepping directly in front of her so that she had to stop. Haydee took the surfboard from Danica's hands and craned forward, right in front of her face. "Danica? Danica, look at me. Are you all right? That was a bad tumble you took out there."

"Stop it," Danica croaked again. She just couldn't take it anymore. All the stares. Haydee's big head looming in front of her all distorted with worry. And now that her ears had cleared she could even pick up some nearby whispers. "Stop it!" she repeated more forcefully.

Haydee's head retracted and she took a step back. "Sorry. I was only seeing if you were okay."

"I'm fine," Danica said shakily. "I just need . . . space."

"Okay. Okay. Why don't we . . . ?"

But Haydee didn't get to finish. Without a word Danica turned and bolted from the beach, running for the red roof of the hotel in the distance.

Somewhere in the back of her mind, she knew she was freaking a bit much, but she didn't care. Her breath was already coming in ragged gasps and in a moment the tears would start up.

And no way was she going to hang around and continue the show for everyone.

"Third place." That's what Zeke had said. Micah got *third place*!

It wasn't good enough to continue on—only the first-place finishers did that. Nor was it good enough to serve as alternate—the second placers did that.

He didn't even get to stand and get photographed by the press like the winner and runner-up. But it was a strong finish. And it was better than he thought he had done.

Micah had only had time to let the news sink halfway in before he saw Danica's wipeout. It looked pretty bad. She walked out of the surf in one piece, but he was still worried. He had never seen her run off like that. She didn't even stick around for her next heat.

Danica was not the type to give up—which meant something was definitely wrong.

So here he was, running back to their hotel to check on her, instead of hanging around the beach and getting congratulated by total strangers while he watched the girls' competition. Not that he minded much. Saying "thanks" over and over again made him feel awkward.

Still . . . *third place*! Even as he worried about Danica, the medal kept thumping against his chest as he jogged, reminding him of his win. He couldn't wait to tell Cassie. Maybe he'd call after he looked in on Danica.

Only . . . would Cassie even think it was a big

deal? She was used to winning tougher, world-class competitions. Third place at a local invitational might not mean much to someone in her league. To hear Bo talk, she was slumming it just hanging around the other campers.

Micah glanced down with a sigh. Suddenly the medal didn't feel all that weighty, and it seemed to have lost some glimmer. Now that he studied it, it actually looked kind of cheap. Even the green ribbon holding it on his neck was frayed slightly.

He entered the lobby and stepped right onto a waiting elevator. The walls inside were covered with mirrors so that everywhere he looked, there he was wearing that medal.

He was proud of it, and he was proud of himself. But he didn't want to feel like some dweeby wannabe around Cassie. Gushing about a third-place win in a third-rate contest might make him look . . .

". . . stupid!"

The elevator had stopped at their floor and the doors had just opened. Sitting in the corridor in front of him, rhythmically thumping the back of her head against the wall, was Danica.

"So"—*thud*—"stupid! I'm so"—*thud*—"freaking stupid!"

"Hey!" Micah cried, bolting out of the lift. "What do you think you're doing?"

Danica's eyes met his, but she kept on lightly banging her head against the cheesy flowered wallpaper. "Sitting," she muttered.

"Uh, yeah. I see that." Micah smiled tentatively but let it drop when she didn't smile back. "So *why* are you just sitting here?"

"I forgot"—*thud*—"my stupid"—*thud*—"key."

Micah was about to ask why she didn't return to the beach for it, but stopped himself. Of course she wouldn't want to go back there. Asking her would have been . . .

". . . stupid," Danica mumbled again.

"Why don't you come into our room for a sec? At least until Haydee comes back? I know it's against the rules, but whatever. You're stranded. She'll understand."

Her eyes swiveled back up to him. For a couple of seconds she didn't say anything, but she at least stopped hammering her head against the wall. "Okay," she said, finally. "Thanks."

Micah let out his breath in relief. It freaked him a little to see Danica like this. Normally she was so strong and collected.

"Here you go," he said, unlocking the door to his and Zeke's room and holding it open for her.

She trudged inside and glanced around as if lost. Then she turned and looked at him. "You won?" she asked, nodding at his medal.

"Oh, uh . . . no," he replied, feeling foolish. "I just got third place." Micah took off the medallion and set it on the dresser. He assumed she didn't want to look at it, and frankly, he didn't either.

"That's great, Micah," she said, sitting on the edge of the bed. "Congratulations."

"Thanks. It's no big deal."

"Sure it is."

He shook his head and sank into a chair. "No, it's not. Not really. But . . . thanks."

"You don't have to do that."

Micah frowned. "What?"

"You don't have to play down your win just for my sake. It's not your fault I sucked out there."

"I . . . I'm not. You didn't. You had an accident. It could have happened to anyone."

83

"*No!* Not to me," she snapped. "I don't let things like that happen to me."

Micah didn't know what to say. It was true she usually managed to avoid mistakes. She was always so . . . ultra aware—so on top of things. For most of last summer he thought she was perfect. But she wasn't. She had flaws and she messed up sometimes. Even she was human.

Of course, pointing that out wouldn't be much of a comfort to her.

"I can't believe I did that," she moaned, shaking her head. "I can't believe I let that hag psych me out."

"Who are you talking about?"

"Nothing." She shut her eyes and lay back on the bed with a sigh. "I screwed up big-time. That's all."

Micah felt like he needed to reassure her in some way. Only he had to be careful not to use the typical "you did great" kind of line. Danica would see right through that, and it would only make her more upset.

"Look . . ." He leaned forward in the chair and clasped his hands, trying not to crack his knuckles the way he tended to do when mulling something over. "Don't be so hard on yourself. It's tougher here. This

84

competition was much harder than Ohana's. Bigger crowds. Bigger deal. The surfers are in a different league . . ."

Danica rose up on her elbows and grimaced. "Easy for you to say. You placed."

"Barely!" He glanced over at his medal and shook his head. "I gave it my all and all I could do was third. You just had some bad luck. If you'd been able to give your best, you'd have smoked them. You'd have won first place easy."

She didn't reply.

"I'm sure even Cassie—"

"Please! I really don't want to talk about her."

Micah frowned. "Fine."

"Look. I appreciate the pep talk, but don't bother. Really. I know what I did wrong."

"What was that?" He couldn't help himself. He had to ask.

Danica let out a long sigh. For a moment he didn't think she'd answer; then she looked straight at him and said, "I let another competitor get to me. And I can't do that in this league. Not if I think I belong here."

Micah leaned back in his chair and stared at the

cottage-cheese pattern on the ceiling. "Don't be so hard on yourself. I let the competitors get to me, too," he said, thinking about Bo.

Danica reached out and nudged him with her foot. "It sucks, doesn't it? It's scary to think that even if you do your best, some people might be better than you."

"Yeah."

They fell silent. Micah could hear the muffled traffic through the closed window, and the ticking of his watch on the nearby dresser. He felt totally separate from the world. It was just him and his thoughts. And Danica.

"But you know what?" Danica sat up and smiled loosely. "Just because someone might be better than you now, doesn't mean they always will be. Right?"

Micah grinned. He wanted badly to hug her— she deserved it for her winning attitude—but he didn't want the weirdness it would bring.

"Yeah," he said. "You're right."

"Go! Go, you little booger!"

The gecko paused as if he'd actually heard and understood Cassie. Then he took off through a small triangular-shaped opening in the wall. His tiny spotted tail gave one last flick, as if waving good-bye, before disappearing from sight.

"Yes!" Cassie raised her right arm in victory. She'd bet herself that the lizard would find that hole. Took him twenty-two minutes. Only . . . now that he was gone, she had nothing left to do.

Now what?

She slowly lowered her arm and tapped out a rhythm on her knees. She couldn't believe it was only a little past noon. It seemed like she'd been there, "recuperating," for hours and hours. Shouldn't it be dark out?

Cassie blew out her breath and glanced around. Let's see . . . she'd already flipped through the fashion magazines Tori brought her. Not that she understood them. She had been halfway through one article about moleskins and softshells before realizing it wasn't about animals. And she still had no idea what zouave leggings were.

How was it possible that a sixteen-year-old girl could be so unaware of such things? Was there something wrong with her? She knew that this stuff wasn't important the way, say, math was important. Or flossing. But she also knew that on a certain level, it did matter. Part of the reason she'd looked forward to this camp was because she wanted to mix it up with "regular" teens. Kids who didn't spend most of their life on a plane or in the ocean, who didn't eat protein bars for lunch or wake up at 4:30 in the morning. Normal young people.

But how could she talk to them if she didn't understand things like fashion, cool TV shows, and the importance of metallics?

Cassie flopped onto her side, keeping her legs crisscrossed so that she resembled the world's laziest yoga practitioner. Her stomach made a little *rrrowl* sound. Even though she was starving, she dared not go find food. Otherwise she'd have to explain her miracle recovery, and Simona would probably have her out teaching surfing before she could even take her first bite.

She felt another twinge in her gut—only this one had nothing to do with hunger. Whenever she thought about how she'd weaseled out of being surf C.I.T., a massive, stomach-kicking guilt passed through her.

Something needed to change. Yes, what had happened to her was horrible and terrifying. Yes, her fear was normal and justified. But when would it stop? She'd come here to get a grip on herself and so far, she'd had hardly any success. Thinking about heading into deep surf chilled her even more than the icy waters of the Pacific.

It was like her head had become separate from her body. She *knew* the chances of being attacked by another shark were close to zero. She *understood* that it had only been a random, freak event. But even though her mind could grasp those things, the rest of her self couldn't. Whenever she swam out to a certain depth . . . or saw an unfamiliar shape in the water . . . her limbs locked up, her breathing became ragged, and her heart sped faster than the beach break. And as soon as that happened, her usually logical brain followed suit—filling with images of large pointed teeth and blood mixing with seawater.

She'd face down her fear—she had to. Only not now. And definitely not when she was supposed to be keeping an eye on some beginner surfers.

Cassie stretched out her arms and legs and let out a yawn. Maybe she should just nap. After all, there wasn't anything else to do.

As soon as she closed her eyes, a sharp sound made her jerk upright. It was coming from the far wall, close to where the gecko had run outside. She leaned off the bed, staring at the hole to see if her little reptilian friend had come back to play some more. But he wasn't there.

The noise came again. She realized now that it couldn't have been the gecko. For one thing, geckos were silent and stealth. For another, this sounded more buglike—a low-pitched whirring, as if a thousand insect wings were flapping at the same time.

Cassie glanced all about. She really hoped there weren't a thousand flying insects coming at her. Was this the time of year for locust swarms?

The buzzing stopped . . . and then started up again. Something was weird. The sound was too regular and rhythmic to be a bug.

She got to her feet and followed the noise. It grew louder as she headed toward Danica's and Sasha's bunks. Again it hummed and this time she fell to her knees and peeked beneath Danica's bed.

And there it was: Danica's cell phone, glowing neon green and shuddering against the woodwork with every ring. It must have slipped down between the mattress and wall and the girl had never noticed. Danica wasn't the neatest of C.I.T.s.

"Great," Cassie muttered. No way could she nap now. Not with that thing chirping every minute.

Bzzzzzzzzzzt! the thing seemed to respond. It was like Danica was mocking her from miles away. Could she have actually planned this?

Bzzzzzzzzzzt! Cassie wanted to toss the thing outside to play with Mr. Gecko. Of course, she couldn't. But maybe if she just turned off the vibrate setting so that it stopped its annoying drone?

Cassie reached beneath the bunk and snatched the small, black, quivering box. Let's see . . . this one was different from hers. It was shinier and sleeker—probably more expensive, too—and with a full-color touch screen. "One text message!" it read, all green and glowing and cheerful. She fumbled with the buttons on the side, hoping she didn't accidentally take a picture of herself. Then a section slid down to reveal even more buttons. Which one would shut it up?

Just then the whole phone pulsed in her grip, startling her.

"Auugh!" she cried. She quickly squeezed the device to avoid dropping it. And suddenly a text message was staring her in the face:

"From: Micah. 14:23 P.M. Message: Howzit? Better? Thx for before. Needed it, too. U left your hair clip in my room, btw. Will sneak it to you later."

Cassie's hands shook so hard, the small black letters seemed to wiggle about. Micah was texting Danica? Why? Weren't they all together, with Haydee and Zeke?

In the far reaches of her mind, Cassie knew it was wrong to read Danica's private message—no matter who it was from. She knew she should put the phone down, walk away, and try to pretend she never saw the text. But she was too shocked, too transfixed to move.

Instead she read the tiny words on the tiny screen over and over and over, as if hoping they might change.

Micah had written "Thx for before." But . . . thanks for what? Did she lend him some sunblock? And why was her hair clip in his room? If it was there, that meant Danica had been there—all relaxing and letting down her blond locks. Had Zeke and Haydee been there, too?

This didn't feel right. The text seemed overly affectionate—intimate even. Like a shared secret. He was thanking Danica . . . for something . . . that happened *in his room.* How could that *not* be bad?

"Don't panic," she told herself. "It's not a big deal."

But it was like her post-shark-attack stress. Even though her mind was open to the idea that there was a reasonable explanation, her hands wouldn't stop shaking and a cold sensation kept shooting through her chest. And the more she read the message, the more Cassie's midsection bunched itself up.

For someone who wasn't sick, her stomach was certainly having a hard time of it today.

After several minutes of staring at the digital screen, she slowly closed the phone, set it on Danica's side table, and padded back to her bunk.

"It's nothing," she kept telling herself as she sprawled out on her mattress and hugged her pillow to her chest. "It doesn't mean anything."

Only . . . her voice didn't sound all that sure of

itself. And once again her body rebelled with several sharp gut pains.

What was it Tori had said about not being able to let go of your ex?

Five

The beach was practically deserted. Of course, Danica had gotten up at 4:00 A.M. for exactly that reason. She didn't want anyone around—not even the fanatical surfers.

It also meant that it was rather dark and chilly. The sun still hadn't risen and only a narrow band of tangerine-colored brightness hugged the horizon. But thanks to the light reflected from shore, she could see well enough.

She paddled out into the surf, gritting her teeth against the cold waves and strong morning current. Nothing would make her turn back. Not even a shark fin. Okay . . . well, maybe a shark fin. (She was determined, not stupid.) But otherwise, absolutely nothing else.

She was not herself. Something had happened

on this trip, and it worried her. She was like . . . Iron Man without his super techno-suit. Or Harry Potter without his wand. Or Jessica Simpson without hair and teeth.

Suddenly and without warning she'd become a much more pathetic version of herself.

Not only did she let some random girl freak her out about a stupid scab—which, by the way, didn't even hurt anymore—she hadn't taken advantage of her alone time with Micah. Back in the hotel room, they'd had such a great moment. It was like old times. Better, even. So why didn't she take the opportunity to win him back? Why didn't she turn on the charm and swoop in before he knew what was hitting him?

Because she was not Danica anymore. At least, not the ultra-confident, untouchable, Camp Ohana Danica.

Maybe this was what happened to Cassie. Maybe the girl hadn't always been so weird and wussy. When Danica first heard that some Super Surf Girl had come to Ohana, she'd practically burst into flames. She'd worked so hard to be a superstar of sorts at that camp, and now a real superstar was there. Only . . . Cassie wasn't like she'd imagined at all. Sure she was pretty, in a regular way, and people seemed to like her—but she wasn't a hotshot. If anything she was kind of boringly normal.

Was that how she'd always been? Or did her little run-in with the shark suck all the special out of her?

Well, no way was this catastrophe of a competition going to fill Danica with lameness. She was going to get her mojo back if she had to steal it.

Danica was out at the breaking point now. The waves were a little rougher than she liked, but nothing she'd never attempted before. She waited for a nice one, rose onto her board, and took off.

Yes! She could do this. She'd conquered so many other things in her life, a racing wave was nothing. All she had to do was . . .

"No!" Suddenly everything felt wrong. She was too tense, and that threw off her entire balance. Danica could feel the board giving out underneath her. She tried to grip it with her feet. She pushed against thin air in a fruitless effort to steady herself. But there was nothing she could do.

And just like that she careened into the breakers, hard—like before.

In the maelstrom of water, bubbles, and grit, her board whacked up against her. And Danica felt something she hadn't felt in a long time: panic.

It was taking too long to resurface, and she didn't have much air left in her. Danica thrashed about, kicking her legs and pushing water out of her path—hoping she was swimming toward the sky and that the wipeout hadn't turned her upside-down.

Finally she broke through the foamy surface and took a long, loud breath.

Stupid, she thought, pulling her board to her and grasping it tightly like a life preserver. It had been stupid to surf on a deserted beach during some of the roughest waves of the day. If something had happened, no one would have been around to help her. Even professional surfers had died doing that.

She was stupid. And she was lame. But at least she was alive.

Danica pointed her board toward the beach and lay down on top of it. She felt weak and breathless, and was thankful the water could at least help carry her back to shore.

And thankful it could hide her tears of frustration.

Let's see . . . Ocean Flower perfume? Nah. That might imply that she smelled bad. A T-shirt? Uh-uh. He didn't want to guess at her size. A beaded wallet? Yeah, right. Nothing says I care about you like a new wallet.

Micah sighed and turned yet another page in the glossy gift-shop catalog someone had slipped beneath their hotel room door during the night (along with the bill). He really wanted to get something for Cassie—something that would prove he'd been thinking about her, something that would make her light up with a smile and—maybe—thank him with a kiss. But what?

A woven pillowcase? A collection of homemade pineapple products? A coconut carved to look like a gorilla? No, no, and no.

What did gorillas have to do with Hawaii, anyway?

The truth was he still didn't know her all that well. He had a strong sense of her (a wonderful, daydream-inspiring sense), but he didn't know her tastes. At least, not like he knew Danica's. After dating Danica for two straight months, he had gotten to know her likes and dislikes. Sort of. Or was it that Danica tended to broadcast her likes and dislikes loudly and clearly and Cassie kept them private?

The thing was, he wanted to get to know Cassie better—much better, in fact. And he was willing to take a few risks. But what if he bought her the absolutely worst gift ever? He didn't want to start it all off with a major screwup.

"I could ask Bo what he thinks," Micah grumbled.

"What?" Zeke asked. He stepped out of the bathroom in his robe, both hands rubbing a towel over his wet hair.

"Nothing. Just talking to myself."

All of a sudden, the door flew open. Both he and Zeke let out tiny shouts of alarm.

Haydee, red-faced and wild-eyed, came barging into the room. "Where's Danica?" she shouted.

It took Micah a few seconds to get over the shock to his system. "I have no idea," he said finally.

"Haydee! You can't just march in here without knocking!" Zeke whined. He gestured to his robe. "I could have been naked."

She glanced over at him and shrugged. "Well, you aren't," she said matter-of-factly. Then she turned back to Micah. "Do you have any idea where she could be?"

Micah shook his head.

"*Aaaargh!*" Haydee made a long, drawn-out noise—a cross between a sigh and a grunt. "We have to be out of here in one hour and she's nowhere to be seen. And she hasn't even started packing! Her stuff is all over the room!"

"I wouldn't worry," Micah said. "She likes to work out stress by, you know, working out. She probably went for a jog or something."

"If she's not back soon, we're leaving without her. She can surf back to Ohana!" Haydee spun around on her sandals and tromped back out, shutting the door with not exactly a slam, but not exactly a polite *click* either.

Micah's heart was still racing. "You don't think Haydee would actually make us leave without Danica, do you?"

"Nah, she's all bark and no action." Zeke pointed toward the door. "But lock up, dude. I can't take another scare like that."

"Sure." As Micah pushed himself off the bed, the gift catalog slid to the floor. After quickly chaining the door, he stooped to pick it back up and saw that the booklet had fallen open to a page near the back.

Micah straightened up and stared closely at the picture. It was a photo of an anklet—a braided band of delicate leather straps adorned with tiny shells arranged in the shape of a flower.

It reminded Micah of Cassie. In fact, he could easily picture it on the end of her long tanned leg. It was perfect.

Or at least, he was pretty sure it was perfect.

A good maybe, anyhow.

Or . . . not.

He sighed and sank back down on his bed. What if buying her a gift was too serious a move? What if it freaked her out? She might say he's moving too fast and back off—which is the opposite of what he hoped would happen.

Micah lay back with a groan, the open catalog forming a little tent around his face. Somehow surfing a monster wave was easier than this.

"Please, Cassie? Please?"

The girl in the mottled pink wet suit, Hannah C. (as opposed to Hannah T., who was in the same bunk), was gesturing out to sea. She was about eleven years old. Not exactly chubby, but big boned and rounded in places.

"The waves are so much better out there," Hannah continued begging. "Just a few more yards? *Pleeeeeeease?*"

Cassie shook her head. "No. Sorry. You'll do great here."

Ben was over his stomach flu. Which meant it was time for Cassie to be over hers. Yesterday evening Simona had come by to check on Cassie and had told her not to worry, that Ben was on his second burger in the mess hall. Obviously it was only a twenty-four-hour bug.

Yay.

So now Cassie was spending her entire morning teaching surfing. No backing out this time. For one thing, she was all out of excuses. And for another, she just couldn't be sneaky about it anymore. Her guilt was getting to be as big and painful as her fear of returning to shark-infested waters. She had to suck it up.

Plus, she wouldn't have been able to handle another extra-long, extra-boring, extra-awful day in the bunkhouse—all alone and with nothing to do but worry herself insane about Micah and Danica . . . Danica and Micah . . . *Micanicah.*

Cassie had agonized over the text message for hours yesterday, squeezing her pillow until it just about disintegrated. She barely even slept through the night. And this morning her stomach felt so knotted, she didn't even try to eat breakfast. So here she was, supposedly cured of her sickness, running on no food and very little rest.

And today Micah and Danica returned.

What should she do? Should she confront him about it? If so, what would she say? That she'd "accidentally" looked at Danica's personal text messages and discovered what was up? And *what*, exactly, was up?

It was clear something had happened. Why else would he refer to her having been in his room? Cassie wanted to come up with some completely plausible and totally innocent explanations, but she couldn't.

Meanwhile Tori's words about exes replayed in her mind like some sort of ghostly recording: *It's never totally over* . . . Cassie couldn't shake the sinking feeling that she'd been horribly naïve to let him leave the island with Danica.

"Come on, Cassie! It's too easy here. Just a few more yards out?" Hannah made her eyes big and round, like a cartoon character pleading for its life.

"Sorry," she replied. "You just aren't ready."

Actually, Hannah was probably ready. But Cassie wasn't. If they swam out to greater depths, she'd probably go all paralyzed with fear. Even if she didn't, she'd be on such ultra-high alert, searching for gray shapes in the water and jumping at every little touch, that she'd be useless as a teacher. Her student might get yanked halfway to Africa in a riptide before Cassie could react.

"Danica lets me," Hannah said with a pout.

"Yeah, well, some people aren't into following rules," Cassie grumbled. "Some people do what they want even if it might hurt others."

She glanced over at her student. Hannah's forehead was all folded up and she was chewing on her bottom lip. She obviously thought Cassie was mad at her.

"Sorry," Cassie said. "I know I'm being strict, it's

just . . . well . . . this is my first day as surf C.I.T. I want to do a good job and follow all the camp regulations. The guidebook says I can't let you into really deep water unless I'm absolutely sure you're ready. And I can't be absolutely sure if I've only been teaching you for forty minutes, right?"

Hannah shrugged. "I guess not."

"I know it looks like fun out there, but remember: It's more dangerous than it looks. Lots more stuff can go wrong, and the farther away from shore you are, the harder it is to get help."

This time the girl glanced over her shoulder at the big waves in the distance. "Yeah. You're right." She sounded seriously disappointed.

"Hey, just because I can't be sure you're ready, doesn't mean everyone will feel that way. When you see Danica," Cassie had to work hard to say the name, "ask her what she thinks. Maybe she'll feel like you can handle it."

"Okay," Hannah said with a smile.

"Great. Now let's catch this next wave and ride it back to shore. Your lesson's over for today."

Time for a break and then only four more sessions to go, Cassie told herself. All in all, she'd handled it better than she thought she would, in spite of her recent distractions. She managed to avoid the deep water. She didn't freeze up. No one died. She'd even succeeded in getting Hannah to stand farther back on her board for better balance. She should be happy, really.

"Hi, Cassie!"

Alexis shouted and waved at her as they waded to shore. She was walking quickly in the direction of her bunk, ready for her late-morning break.

Cassie raised her hand in greeting. She was just about to say "hi" back when Alexis turned her head and her pretty, twisted metal hairclip glinted in the sunlight.

Once again, an image of Micah's text haunted Cassie's mind. *"U left your hair clip in my room, btw . . ."*

Cassie's stomach tightened and it took all her muscle power to continue heading toward the beach. She really wished she could get just five straight minutes of normal thought.

"Your hair clip . . . in my room . . . my room . . ."

That phrase was bad enough—but it wasn't the

real horrible part. The next sentence really made her gut clench: *"Will sneak it to you later."*

It was the word *sneak* that really made her feel shaky. It implied that something dishonest was going on. And it made it impossible for her to think up other, less scary reasons why Danica would have been there.

"Thanks a lot, Cassie," Hannah said.

Cassie snapped out of her thoughts and was surprised to find herself on dry sand.

"I hope you get to teach me again soon," Hannah went on. "Sorry I was such a grouch."

"No problem. Sorry I was so . . . careful." She looked out at the breakers. They were perfect—clean, even, just the right size. If she'd been her old self, she would have agreed to let Hannah surf out there. In fact, she might have suggested it first.

This had to change. She had to start *making* it change.

"No biggie," the girl replied. "I know you were just doing your job. Bye!"

The girl headed in the direction of the cabins, passing Tori, who was jogging straight toward Cassie.

"Hey! You're better!" she said.

Cassie nodded. "I am."

"Cool! We can sunbathe." She grabbed the rolled-up beach towel she had tucked under her arm and began to spread it out on the sand.

"Uh . . . Tor. This isn't your free class. Aren't you supposed to be with your group?"

"It's cabin clean time. But Madison said she'd straighten my area for two weeks in exchange for my eyelet Juicy Couture shirt—which is so last year anyway. So . . . *bonus* free hour!" She sat down on her oversize towel and patted the space next to her.

Cassie could only shake her head and plop down beside her. Leave it to Tori to find ways around all the rules.

"So . . .?" Tori flashed her a knowing smile. "Aren't you excited?"

"About . . .?"

"Micah's coming back later today! Have you heard anything?"

The sound of Micah's name made her gut cramp up so fiercely, she almost balled up into a fetal position. Cassie could feel her cheeks grow pink. "What do you mean? Heard what?"

"Have you heard anything about the competition?"

"Oh! No. I haven't heard anything about that."

"Well, you'll find out soon. They should be here in a few hours." Tori gave Cassie's wrist an excited squeeze—the same intensity as the squeezing in Cassie's midsection.

She wondered if she should share her dilemma about the text message. After all, Tori was a self-admitted expert on relationships. But Cassie wasn't even sure she could accurately explain the situation without incriminating herself as a world-class snoop. Plus she didn't fully understand it herself.

So instead she watched her cousin start pulling items out of her big, expensive, and apparently bottomless bag. Magazines, nail polish, a bottle of Vitamin Water, lip gloss, compact, hairbrush, a spray bottle of something, two scrunchies, and a chocolate-peanut butter energy bar. The last item she held out to Cassie.

"Want it? I'm still full from breakfast."

Maybe she should eat something. Maybe that would quell the churning in her stomach. It would be ironic if she actually got sick after pretending to be ill yesterday. Probably serve her right.

"Okay. Thanks, Tor." Cassie took it and started opening the wrapper. "And thanks for yesterday, too. Sorry you got kicked out of my room. That was really nice of you to share all that stuff with me."

"Hey, that's what I'm here for. To make your life better." She grinned her hundred-watt smile. Then she leaned back and spritzed her neck with whatever the spray bottle contained.

Cassie studied her cousin. She might have been half-joking, but Tori spoke the truth. She did make her feel better. Camp would have been much more boring and confusing if it wasn't for her. There was just something about Tori that comforted Cassie. It was as if she had so much confidence, some of it *had* to ooze off of her and onto Cassie.

Wait a minute . . . that's what she needed to do! She needed to hit the waves with Tori. Maybe that would make her feel strong enough to face her fears. At sea *and* on land.

"Hey, Tor," she began, in between bites. "You want to go surfing today—during your *real* free hour?" She tried to sound matter-of-fact. She didn't want

Tori to take this on as a project. Otherwise instead of being fun and bubbly and distracting Cassie from her fears, she'd turn into super nursemaid again—like yesterday. As it was, Cassie was barely keeping back panicky tears. Too much doting kindness would make her blubber for sure.

"No, thanks. I want to darken my legs today. I'm like the palest girl in my bunk—except for Lisette. And she's from Minnesota!"

"Aw, come on." Cassie nudged her leg with her foot. "It'll be fun."

"No. It's your thing. I'm really not that good."

"You just need practice. I'll work with you."

"Sorry." Tori lay back and put on her sunglasses. "I'm too depressed."

Cassie scrunched up her face. "Depressed?" She didn't seem at all upset. In fact, *depressed* would be about the last word she would have chosen to describe her cousin's mood. Cassie was the one in a funk—not her.

"Yeah," Tori replied with a sigh. "Eddie found someone. I was wrong about Larkin Fennell, but not this girl. Madison told me that Gina told her that he's asking her to the dance."

"Dance? What dance?"

"Oh yeah. You were sick yesterday. They announced it at general assembly. It's called the Tiki Dance. Apparently they have it every year."

"So . . . you're depressed because you wanted to go with Eddie?"

Tori raised her glasses in order to shoot her a look. "No. I don't want to go with him. I just don't want him to go with someone else. If he has someone new and I don't, that makes me look bad. It'll be like . . . he won."

Cassie bit off a large hunk of protein bar and chewed it slowly, without tasting it. She really wished she understood the strange, subtle rules of relationships. But listening to Tori made her feel like she'd just gotten out of her diaper-wearing stage. Why did everything have to be so complicated?

Cassie looked out at the ocean. An hour of free surf had just begun for the older guys and several of the experienced kids were out hitting those perfect waves.

When it came down to it, surfing was the only simple thing in her life—the only thing with clear rules and consequences. It was all about learning to read your body. Over time you figure out to how tiny movements and shifts in weight can help with balance, speed, and form. It was just you, water, and the laws of physics. You didn't need anyone else.

Maybe that was why Cassie was good at it. At least, when she could actually bring herself to do it.

She forced herself to finish the energy bar and then leaned back on her hands, taking in the view of the surfers. They were having a great time. Of course they were. Conditions were ideal and they were fearless—just like she used to be.

One guy in particular knew what he was doing. She could tell he was still a novice, but he had the instinct, that ability to listen to and command his body.

"Man, he's good," Cassie exclaimed as she watched him.

"Who?" Tori rose up on her elbows.

"I don't know his name. He's out in the surf. The one in red trunks."

"Hmmm." Tori sat up and raised her glasses. "I don't know him either. But I want to."

Cassie smiled. Guess Tori wasn't "depressed" anymore.

"You know what?" Tori turned and grinned at her. "Maybe I'll take you up on some surfing practice after all."

Six

Cassie had never been so happy to rack up a surfboard and walk away from a beach. The sand felt extra soft beneath her feet. The thatched cabins in the distance looked extra quaint and cozy. Even the palm trees seemed to stretch out their fronds for a reassuring hug.

She'd gotten through surf C.I.T. duty just fine. No shark attacks. No injuries. Not even a blister. But her students had flashed an assortment of disappointed looks whenever she nixed their suggestion to go out into deeper waters. They were both let down and totally shocked. She could tell they'd thought getting taught by the pro surfer girl would be amazingly cool—in fact, one of them pleaded with her to demonstrate some moves. Then they discovered she was a big lame-o.

Of course, it wasn't just imaginary sharks that made her a big dud. Micah's text message to Danica still kept popping into her mind without warning, making her forget what she was doing.

In just a few hours they'd be back at Ohana. And what then? Would Micah dump her? *Could* he dump her? After all, they never really got a chance to be an official couple.

Or maybe he wouldn't dump her. Maybe whatever happened in Oahu was just an ex thing, and he'd act like everything was cool.

But could she deal with that?

"Cassie! Cassie, are you okay?" Charlie suddenly ran up beside her. She stopped as he gripped his knees and took a deep breath.

"Yeah, I'm fine. Why?" A cold tingle came over her. Did *he* know about Micah and Danica? Is that why he was asking?

"'Cause I called your name, like, ten times," he said, still panting slightly.

"Sorry. What's up?"

"Simona sent me to get you. You're relieved from kitchen prep duty."

"Oh. Good." That was the best news she'd

received all day, but she couldn't seem to muster up much enthusiasm. It just didn't seem to matter in the scheme of things. Not when her boyfriend (or whatever he was) still texted his ex-girlfriend and her whole life was going to have to be revised due to constant crippling fear.

"Yeah, she wants you to do something else instead," Charlie went on.

"What's that?"

"You're supposed to come with me to the old clubhouse. She wants us in charge of planning this Friday's Tiki Dance."

"What?" Cassie slumped with disappointment. "Why me?"

Charlie shrugged. "Beats me. She just told me to tell you. I thought you'd be glad to get out of kitchen duty."

"Yeah, I guess." Cassie didn't want to tell him that she was much more comfortable peeling potatoes than she was planning an evening's entertainment. She'd only been to a few beach parties—corporate-sponsored events that were more about shaking hands and making deals than having fun. And she'd only attended one actual boy-girl dance before—one of the suckiest nights of her life.

So how, exactly, was she supposed to plan one?

"Come on. They're waiting," Charlie said, heading down another path.

"Who's waiting?"

He turned around and flashed her a confused look. "The dance committee."

"Right. I just . . . I didn't realize they were meeting this very second."

They silently trudged down the part-dirt, part-sand trail, startling a couple of nearby birds. Cassie tried to think of ways to back out, but her mind was too sleep-deprived and Micah-obsessed to come up with anything usable.

Charlie, she noticed, also seemed to be mulling something over.

"So . . . you'll be going to the dance with Micah, huh?" he asked eventually.

Cassie paused, startled by the question. The now-familiar ache in her gut switched to a higher setting. "Um, maybe." She wondered if she should open up to Charlie. Her worry over Micah's text to Danica was like an enormous boulder inside her—constantly hurting and weighing her down. Maybe she should just . . . let it out?

She glanced over at him. Charlie looked so upright and decent in his khaki shorts and checkered short-sleeve shirt buttoned almost to the collar. He was such a nice guy. Would he even understand why she looked at the private message? Would he think she was an awful person for having read it? And was she?

Then again, maybe she was better off not telling anyone. At least not yet.

"Aw, come on," Charlie said. "You guys are going together. That's a given."

Don't bet on it. "Yeah, well . . . he doesn't even know about it yet. He may not feel up for it after the trip and stuff."

"So . . . do you know if . . ." He fell silent, his mouth moving soundlessly for a few seconds. Finally he swallowed hard and continued. "Do you know if Andi is going with anyone?"

Cassie was overcome with sympathy and understanding. Poor guy. "I don't really know. I'm sorry."

He looked so disappointed, he actually seemed to shrink a bit. "That's okay."

"You know, you should ask her."

This time Charlie looked startled. "Ah . . .

no. No, no, no." He shook his head vigorously.

"You should! Come on. Why not?"

"Because she'd probably say no. And then the rest of the summer would be ruined. And we haven't even made it to July."

"Why are you so sure she'll say no?"

Charlie stopped walking and stared out over the terrain to the sea. He let out a long sigh and shook his head again. "Because I'm me. And she's . . . she's amazing."

Cassie felt so bad for him. She wanted to pat his head and scratch him under the chin the way she did to her neighbor's old sad-eyed Labrador, Bart.

And she knew what it was like to be paralyzed with doubt.

"Anyway. Whatever." Charlie suddenly looked embarrassed. "We should go." He spun around on his flip-flops and started walking again, even faster than before.

"Okee-dokey," she said, falling into step behind him.

Tori was right. They had to help the guy. Cassie wasn't exactly sure how someone as mixed up as her could be of any help, but she had to try.

Cassie sat on a tabletop next to Charlie looking over the crowd. In her hands were a notebook and pencil. As cohead of the Tiki Dance's organizing committee, she figured it would come in handy as well as make her look official. But so far she'd just been holding it face up in her lap like a mini shield.

It turned out that everyone who showed for the voluntary dance-planning meeting was female, most of them from Tori's bunkhouse, and the other girl C.I.T.s, like Sasha and Sierra. Andi was also there, which made Charlie all sad-eyed and fidgety.

Cassie kept glancing at the large clock mounted on the opposite wall. Like a bomb, it seemed to be loudly ticking down to the time when Micah would reappear. So she, too, was squirmy and distracted.

Together they were the most useless dance planners ever.

"Why can't we have it on the beach?" Sierra was asking.

"Simona wants to have it in the mess hall where there's better lighting, and therefore, better supervision," Charlie explained.

"Can it be formal?" Sasha asked.

"Can we carve a watermelon to look like a swan?" Gina asked.

"Look, guys." Charlie's low voice cut through the murmuring. "I don't think Simona wanted us to come up with all sorts of crazy ideas. The Tiki Dance is just a regular dance."

"Yeah. We should probably focus on stuff like what kind of music to play and what types of food to serve," Cassie added—feeling like she should say something.

"You can use the music on my iPod," Sasha suggested. "I have about one hundred and fifty songs."

"I have three hundred songs," Sierra said.

"Man, I have only ninety-something," Esme grumbled.

"I have about ten thousand," Charlie remarked.

Everyone stared at him open-mouthed.

"What? I have an eighty-gig player," he explained. "Sue me for being a music lover."

"Well, I guess that solves the whole music dilemma," Cassie remarked, sneaking her two-hundredth look at the clock. *Let's get this over with.*

"It doesn't solve it!" Sierra pouted. "What if we don't like his stuff?"

"Yeah," echoed Sasha.

"Guys, I have, like, everything. And if I don't have something you want, I can get it. I'm at the computer each day," Charlie pointed out.

"Okay, then." Cassie raised her hands for silence. "How about if everyone writes down ten songs—"

"Only ten?"

"Okay, *twenty* songs that you really want included in the mix and hand them over to Charlie." She waited for any additional grumbles, but none came. "Which leaves food. Who wants to help come up with a list of snacks?"

"Pizza's always good," suggested Madison.

"But it's a *tiki* party," Andi said. "Shouldn't we have luau food? Like . . . I don't know . . . roasted pig?"

"Hey! Some of us are vegetarian!" cried someone in the back.

Tori stood and raised her hands in a quieting gesture. "People, listen! Remember, many of us will be on dates. That means we don't want anything messy like big, drippy pizza. We also don't want anything greasy, or crumbly, or too hard to hold, or that leaves stuff in your teeth, or gives you bad breath . . ."

"Um . . . doesn't that pretty much rule out all food?" Charlie quipped.

"Little finger snacks are okay," Tori said, sitting back down.

"Like those tiny little quiches?"

"Ooh! I like canapés. You can get some good frozen ones."

Suddenly everyone was talking. Their jabbering voices melded together into one big, incomprehensible sound. Tori, having made her point, came and sat down beside Cassie.

"This seems to be going well," she said.

Cassie glanced hard at her, trying to decide if she was being sarcastic or not. But apparently she was sincere.

"We've got to wrap this up," Cassie said. "I have to . . . do stuff." According to the clock, Micah would be back at camp in slightly less than two hours. That didn't give her much time to dress and primp—and grow a backbone.

She hoped to look her absolute best when he

125

arrived. She wanted him to stare at her the same way he did when he was leaving—when they kinda-sorta-almost kissed. She wanted him to reassure her everything was the same.

If she could make herself face him.

"I'll end it." Charlie curled his hands around his mouth. "Okay, listen up! Who wants to be on the committee to plan and set up snacks?"

Six hands shot into the air. Cassie, fairly sure of their names, wrote them down. At least now she had something on her pad.

"Great. Thanks," Charlie called out. "You guys get together and plan. Just be sure and give us the list before Simona goes on her grocery run tomorrow. The rest of you are free to go."

The room erupted into noise and activity as some people left and others gathered together to discuss food options.

"Hey, Charlie!" Andi was making her way through the room toward them. Cassie watched as he sat up extra straight, his right hand absently smoothing his hair. "Here you go," she said as she reached their table. She handed a piece of paper over to Charlie. "Here's my list of twenty songs."

Charlie grasped the sheet and smiled at her. "Yes."

"Yes?" Andi repeated, looking confused.

"I mean . . ." Charlie blinked rapidly and shook his head a little, as if snapping himself out of a trance. "I mean, yes, I have these."

Andi seemed even more baffled. "But you haven't even looked at the list yet."

"Yeah, but . . . um . . . we have the same tastes so . . . I'm sure I have them. If I don't, I'll get them. Because . . . because we have the same tastes."

"Oo-kayyy." Andi tilted her head, as if staring at Charlie from a new angle might make him more understandable. "Well . . . thanks." She glanced at Tori and Cassie. "Sorry, I've got to run, guys. I told Simona I'd do a surprise inspection of the *nene* bunk. They're such slobs, they have cockroaches moving in with them. Bye!"

She twirled about and headed out the door at her trademark half-jog speed. As soon as her auburn curls bounced out of sight, Charlie let out a small moan and fell over sideways until he was slumped against the wall.

"Are you okay?" Cassie asked.

"I'm fine," Charlie mumbled. "I'm a complete idiot. But otherwise, I'm fine. Thanks."

Tori gave him a gentle shove on the shoulder. "Why didn't you ask her to the dance?"

"Come on. You saw me. I could barely speak English. How was I supposed to ask her out?" he whined. "Besides, she would have said no. And maybe laughed at me."

"How do you know that if you don't even try?" Tori demanded. "It's, like, less than ten words. I think. Let's see . . . will-you-go-with-me-to . . ." she mumbled, counting off on her fingers. "Oh well. Anyway, it's not many."

"Look. I appreciate your little pep talk and all but . . . I'm beyond help. Just go. Save yourselves. Leave before my lameness rubs off on you."

"Tell him, Cassie." Tori was now shoving her shoulder. "Tell him it's so worth it to just go for it."

"Um . . . ." Cassie wasn't sure how to respond. She didn't exactly "go for it" with Micah. In fact, she made so many mistakes, it was a miracle he didn't give up on her completely. Of course, he might have already. The text message wasn't the best of signs . . .

Then again, she was pretty certain that Charlie and Andi could get things right.

"Yeah," she finally replied. "It's so worth it."

"Thanks anyway, guys. Now if you'll excuse me, I have to go bang my head against a palm tree." Charlie slid off the table and shuffled out the door, his shoulders slumped in defeat.

So much for helping him, Cassie grumbled inwardly. The guy looked even sadder than before. Even more evidence that love sucked.

"Don't worry. We'll get them together," Tori said as if reading her mind. "In the meantime, how about a quick surf lesson?"

"Now?" Cassie glanced up at the clock.

"Well, yeah. I mean, you're done coaching the surfers and the meeting is over. What else is on your schedule?"

"Nothing. But Micah . . ."

"Micah won't be back for a while. What are you going to do? Go get your hair done? If I know you, you'll spend ten minutes primping, and an hour and a half pacing around."

She had a point. Cassie probably would drive herself crazy—make that craz*ier*—that final hour. Micah would return to find her a quivering, stammering mess.

Maybe she was better off taking out all her nervous energy on the surf. Plus, with Tori with her, she could work on overcoming her fears.

"Please?" Tori begged.

"Okay," she relented. "But only a quick lesson."

"Here we are!" Zeke called out, motioning to the left. They could see Camp Ohana's cluster of cabins in the distance.

Micah's stomach seemed to jump into his chest cavity. *Finally!* He couldn't wait to see Cassie.

He would tell her about his third-place win and she'd whoop loudly and say how proud she was of him.

He would tell her he met Bo and she would roll her eyes and talk about what a jerk he was.

He would give her the anklet and she would gasp in surprise. Then she would hug him. Then they would kiss . . .

At least, that was what he *hoped* would happen.

"Home sweet home!" Haydee sang out as Zeke drove past the front gates of the camp.

Beside him, Danica grumbled something he couldn't make out.

Micah's legs jiggled and he nervously patted his left pants pocket, where the anklet was stored. Wouldn't be long now.

He'd felt pretty sure of himself when he bought the anklet. Out of all that stuff in the catalog and on the souvenir shop shelves, it was the only thing that seemed like Cassie. But . . . what if she hated it? Or what if it freaked her out that he bought her a gift?

He couldn't afford a mistake. Now that he'd met Bo, he fully realized that Cassie was different from most girls. She'd seen the world and accomplished so much. The last thing he wanted was for her to think of him as beneath her.

Bo.

Just thinking about that guy made Micah sit forward and give the door handle a tight, white-knuckled squeeze. He was supposed to tell Cassie "hi" from the dude. But he didn't want to. He didn't want her to have an image of him and Bo in her mind at the same time—because he knew he'd be the less interesting, less talented, and possibly less worthy of the two visions.

"And there's our welcome wagon!" Zeke called out as he steered the van into a parking space.

Micah could barely breathe. Glancing out the windshield, he could see campers running from all directions to greet them. *Here goes* . . .

He opened the van's side door and stepped out onto the gravel parking lot. People were rushing toward them, all of them silhouetted against the descending sun.

"Hey! How'd it go?"

"Welcome back! How was it?"

"Hey, you guys! How'd you do?"

Micah squinted at each of the talking shadow figures, but he didn't recognize anyone. At last Ben stepped forward into his field of vision.

"Hey, dude!" He grasped Micah's hand and gave it a firm shake, then pulled him close for a back slap. "Tell us about the contest, man! Simona wouldn't give us the results. She said we had to wait for you guys to get back."

"Well . . ." Micah glanced around for Cassie. He'd wanted her to be the first person he told. Where was she? "I placed third," he said eventually. No need to be all evasive. Ben would just hear about it from Zeke or Haydee anyway.

"All right!" Ben high-fived him and socked him in the shoulder. "Way to go, man! And how about Danica?"

"Um, she . . . She, um . . ." Micah really wasn't sure how to explain it.

"She did her best," Haydee cut in as she climbed out of the van's passenger seat.

"What they're trying to say," Danica walked toward them, her chin held high, "is that I didn't place. I lost."

"Oh. Well . . ." Ben seemed suddenly uncomfortable. "I'm sure you rocked it."

"No, I didn't." Danica flashed him a somewhat scary smile.

"Hey, guys! You're back!" Charlie suddenly flew into their little group. He gave Micah a friendly slap on the shoulder (which hurt much less than Ben's). "How was it?"

"Micah got a third-place finish," Ben told him.

Charlie looked at Micah and broke into a huge grin. "You did? That's awesome, man!"

"Thanks. Um, hey. Have you seen Cassie?"

"Yeah. I just passed her. She's out surfing with her cousin."

Micah's stomach dropped back down into place. In fact, it seemed to plummet into his shoes. Cassie wasn't there to greet him? What did that mean?

"So what about you?" Charlie turned his big, clueless smile toward Danica. "How did you—?"

"Hey, guys," Haydee interrupted. She plopped one heavy hand on Charlie's shoulder and the other on Ben's and steered them toward the back of the van. "I need you two to help me unload all this luggage and gear . . ."

As they walked off, Micah scanned the rest of the assembled onlookers. But Charlie was right. Cassie wasn't there.

"Surfing, huh?" Danica walked up beside him. "Ouch. And here I thought she was so into you." She shot him a sympathetic look, made a little *tsk-tsk* sound, and trotted away, shaking her head.

Micah took a deep breath. *Don't let it get to you*, he told himself. Danica was just being Danica.

She'd been competitive with Cassie since she got here and loved any opportunity to make her look bad. Besides, it was obvious she was still upset about her wipeout.

Still, he had to wonder. Where exactly was he on Cassie's list of priorities?

***

"Tori, I think it's getting late. The sun is really low. We should head back."

"Already?"

"Yeah. Simona wanted us all to be near the entrance to greet those guys when they return." Cassie couldn't bring herself to say that *she* wanted to be there. She still wasn't sure if she did or not.

"I know, I know. But just one more run? Please?" Tori whined as she hugged her borrowed Camp Ohana surfboard and bobbed in the baby waves. "I'm really starting to nail it."

Cassie had to admit, Tori was right about that. She was getting really good really fast. Seemed like whenever a cute boy was a motivating factor, there was nothing her cousin couldn't accomplish.

It was kind of annoying, really. Here Cassie was, a so-called "pro" surfer, and she was the most freaked out about heading into deep water.

Being out there with Tori had helped a little. She still wasn't able to head out to the big beautiful waves, but at least she wasn't stuck in the wash. Her stance was way too tense and her timing was off. If someone had been watching from the shore, they would have assumed she was an extremely good *beginning* surfer instead of an award-winning, corporate-sponsored pro competitor.

But at least she was surfing. If she'd been able to push her worries about Micah aside, she might have actually had fun.

The sky was darkening and the water was getting that metallic shimmer of early evening. Cassie glanced at the cabin roofs in the distance. Was Micah back yet? When she'd asked Simona permission to give Tori an off-hours lesson, the head counselor had made two things clear: 1) that it was Cassie's responsibility to make sure Tori and all camp equipment made it back safely, and 2) that she expected them to greet their Ohana surf competitors when they returned.

Thanks, Simona. Cassie had already been stressed about seeing Micah and Danica again. Now she was almost as stressed about the possibility of *not* seeing them.

"Come on, Tor!" she shouted. Her left foot jiggled nervously, stirring up tiny eddies of sandy water.

She watched as Tori grabbed another wave and whooped as it hurtled her toward shore. A beautiful, near-perfect ride. If this kept up, her cousin would be better than her at absolutely everything: boys, relationships, fashion, friends, *and* surfing.

Right at that moment, Tori checked her balance, leaned too far to the right, and went tumbling into the water. The sight made Cassie feel a tiny bit better. Okay, so maybe Tori had a ways to go before she was better at the sport.

Cassie saw Tori's head come up and paddled toward her.

"Okay. Good one. Now it's really time to go back."

"You're right," she said, breathlessly. "Micah will probably be here any second. I know you can't wait." She flashed a meaningful smile.

Micah. Just the sound of his name brought back the harsh clawing sensations in Cassie's abdomen.

She wanted to see him—and yet she didn't. On the one hand, all this waiting and wondering had to stop. Once she saw him, she could look him straight in the eye and search for any signs of guilt or deception.

But what if she didn't like what she found?

"Uh-oh . . . where's my board?" Tori asked, twisting this way and that in the water.

Cassie frowned. "What do you mean, 'where's my board?'"

"It's gone."

"What are you talking about? Did the leash break?"

"I don't know."

"Or did you not strap it right?"

"I don't know," Tori repeated. "It just . . . came off."

Cassie let out a frustrated grunt. "Great! Simona's going to be so mad at us!"

"She'll understand."

"Not if we lose the board, she won't. The only reason they let me borrow it outside of free surf hours is because I'm a C.I.T. If we lose it, *I* have to pay for it!" She slapped the water angrily and the spray hit her right in the face.

Tori stared at her for a moment. "I'm sorry, Cass. I'm really, really sorry. Look, I know you want to go get spiffed up a little and meet Micah. You go on. I'll find the board."

Cassie blew out her breath and stared at the sunset. "No, I'm sorry. Sorry I lost my cool."

"Seriously, Cass. You go. I'm the one who lost the board so I should look for it."

"No!" Cassie shook her head. "It's getting dark and the water is rough. No one should be out here by themselves. Let me see if I can spot it." She straddled her board and sat up, scanning the nearby waves.

"Hey, Cass?"

"Yeah?"

"Is something bothering you? I mean . . . that wasn't all about the board, was it?"

Cassie stared openmouthed at Tori. In addition to her other skills, reading minds seemed to be something else the girl was good at.

"What gave you that idea?"

"I know you. Something's up. Something's been

up for a while, hasn't it? Does it have to do with Micah?"

"No." Even Cassie could hear the lie in her voice. Why was she in such denial, anyway? Maybe if she let out her worries, she could also let out that heavy, high-pressured feeling in her chest.

Besides, Tori was good at analyzing relationships. It could very well be her strongest talent.

"Okay, fine. There is something. But it's probably stupid."

Cassie leaned forward on her board as Tori grabbed hold of the nose and floated along with her. Taking a deep breath, she made herself describe what happened in the bunkhouse while she was sick— about the text message and its weird wording.

Once she'd finished pushing the words up out of her, Cassie had to admit the heaviness was also gone. But in its place was a crushed, worn-out feeling.

Tori sighed. "Okay, yeah. It does sound kind of bad," she said, nodding slightly. "But maybe there's a completely good reason for the message."

Cassie raised her eyebrows. "Like what?"

"Well . . . I don't know . . . maybe he broke

something and Danica covered for him and that's why he was thanking her."

"But why was she in his room?"

"Beats me." Tori shrugged. "But I wouldn't freak out until you know more. It could be no big deal."

"I don't know, Tor. I just . . . don't want to end up feeling like a total fool. I mean, you're the one always talking about how it's never really over between exes."

Tori's forehead crumpled. "Oh god. Sorry. You shouldn't listen to me." She reached out and squeezed Cassie's arm. "It'll be okay. Really. You'll see." Her tone was all hushed and sweet—as if Cassie were a scared five-year-old. Hearing it, Cassie's vision automatically blurred and her throat felt tight and bulgy.

"Yeah, well . . ." Cassie swallowed hard and blinked back the wetness in her eyes. So stupid to be this frantic over a boy. A boy she barely knew. "But what if it isn't okay?" she asked, her voice barely a whisper.

Tori socked her shoulder gently. "Then you should totally get into someone new. Like me! I was all gloomy until I saw . . . Surf Guy."

"You still don't know his name?"

"I'm working on it. The point is that he made me forget Eddie. And there are tons of other cool guys around for you, too!"

Cassie didn't want to bring up the fact that there were far fewer C.I.T.s and counselors (guys her age) than there were campers (guys Tori's age). Or that the thought of going after another member of the male species made her feel tired and extra stomachache-y. Tori might be ultra confident and skilled when it came to the opposite sex, but not Cassie. It was a miracle she got Micah's attention as long as she did.

"Hey, look! There it is!" Tori motioned to a spot several yards up the beach where the yellow surfboard was bobbling near the shore.

They paddled toward the beach, angling themselves toward the stray board.

"Hey, Cass?" Tori's voice took on that super-understanding pitch again.

Cassie hesitated a second before replying. "Yeah?"

"I'm not saying he did anything wrong . . . in fact, I'd bet he didn't . . . but even if it turns out he

142

was a jerk, you've still got to face him and get the whole story. Otherwise you'll always be wondering. It'll make you feel better, I promise."

"I don't know." The very thought made Cassie want to turn completely around and start heading out to sea.

"Hey, you're the one with nothing to hide. You've got nothing to lose," Tori pointed out. "In fact, you don't even have to say anything. Just stare him down and make him squirm. Trust me. It'll make you feel *much* better."

"Yeah, I guess so." Cassie had to admit she at least deserved some answers.

"No. No 'guess.' Promise me."

"I promise."

Seven

"Tori! You're heading out too far!" Cassie cupped her hands and yelled at her cousin's fiercely paddling backside.

This was so déjà vu.

Only ten hours earlier, they were in this exact spot doing this exact thing. Nothing had changed. Cassie had tried to find Micah, but couldn't. Then she got cornered by Simona, who wanted to know why she and Tori hadn't greeted their fellow campers. After Cassie explained about the lost board, Simona wanted a summary of the dance committee meeting. Once the conversation finally ended, it was time for lights out.

She didn't even get to face Danica. Her rival had turned in early and was already in her bed facing the wall when Cassie returned to the bunkhouse.

Probably wiped out from the trip. And all that making out with Micah.

"Cassie, look!" Tori had caught up to a massive wave and pulled herself upright. Her face was practically shining with joy.

"Excellent!" Cassie called back. "Watch your—"

Just then Tori's board started to quaver. Tori tried to steady herself, but once again leaned too far to the right and crashed into the surf. Thankfully, the board didn't come unleashed this time.

"You're doing it again," she shouted as soon as Tori's head broke the surface. "You're—"

"I know! I know!" Tori sputtered a bit and pushed her hair out of her eyes. "I go too far to the right."

"But that was awesome, really. Especially for your level. Don't be in too much of a hurry. Stay closer to shore until you get better with your balance." *And until I get used to the deep water again*, she added silently.

Cassie had managed to make a little more progress that morning. She'd headed out a little farther than the previous day. Actually it was only a few inches, but it was an improvement. Tori was pushing her to go to real shark-patrolling depths. But just feeling the icy water on her dangling feet brought back too many bad memories.

"Really. Don't push it. You have plenty of time," Cassie added. "Deal?"

"Deal," Tori grumbled.

Cassie glanced back at the beach. The camp was waking up and people were out of their bunks, heading to the beach or the mess hall. "That's probably enough for today. We should head back."

"Already?"

"Yeah. You don't want to tire yourself. And besides . . ." Cassie let out a sigh and stared down at the water's shimmery surface. "I kind of don't want to be here when Micah and Danica show up for their surf C.I.T. duties."

"That's not for a while," Tori pointed out. "And besides, you told me you'd try to talk to him. You promised."

"Yeah, I know. But not here. Not with Danica lurking around like some . . . shark."

"Then where? When?"

"I don't know." Cassie tried to imagine the perfect setting for meeting back up with Micah.

It had to be someplace where they could be alone, someplace where she could get close enough to read his face without squinting. Someplace where there were no rocks, shells, and other objects she could hurl—just in case she was tempted. "Let's just go, okay? Maybe I'll figure it out over breakfast."

"No way. We *definitely* can't leave now." Tori suddenly straightened her posture and smoothed her wet hair with her left hand.

"Why?"

"'Cause look who just showed up." Tori nodded toward shore where Hunky Surfer Guy was just heading into the waves with his board.

"Okay . . . but why should I be here?"

"Because you have to. I don't want to be out here by myself. *Please*?" Tori said, making big pleading, baby deer eyes. "You don't have to be right there with me. Just stay nearby in case I need you."

"Oh, all right." While Tori headed back toward the breakers, Cassie paddled about, pretending to relax and sun herself on her board. Tori managed to grab a couple of good waves and Cassie could tell that Hunky Surfer Guy noticed.

"She's good," she overheard him say to a pal as she drifted nearby.

Yep, she's good all right, Cassie thought. Tori was acting like she had no idea she was being watched. As if all she cared about was making some great rides.

Probably the perfect path to a surfer boy's heart.

"Hey, Cassie!"

A familiar voice called out from behind. It crashed over her like a freezing wave.

Cassie braced herself and then slowly pivoted about. Sure enough, there on the shore, looking even more incredible than she remembered, was Micah.

Oh no. Not now. Please. I'm not ready.

"Hi," she called back. She felt foolish just floating there like a piece of driftwood.

Now what? He was too far for her to really see his expression. So much for reading it. Should she go up to him? Maybe. Or would that look too eager and weak?

No matter. Micah was now wading into the water toward her, surfboard in tow. She sat up on her board and tried to steady her breathing. Her heart was threatening to burst out of her and go bouncing over the waves like a skipping stone.

She could see his face now. Cassie was surprised to see that he was smiling—although he looked sort of nervous. His forehead was bunched in the middle and his bottom lip was kind of tucked into his mouth. Oh no. Why? What was he so worried about?

"Hey," he said as he came within a couple feet.

"Hey," she said back. Her lips automatically curled upward. Stupid lips. She shouldn't make this easy for him. She wanted to keep him guessing—just like she was.

"So . . . um . . . missed you yesterday. When we got back."

"Yeah. Sorry. I was giving Tori a surf lesson and we lost track of time."

"Surf lesson, huh?" His smile seemed to slide right off his face.

Cassie suddenly felt the need to explain. "We lost her board and it took forever before we found it. You know how they are about the equipment."

"Yeah." His grin came back, but not entirely.

For a moment they simply treaded water and nodded at each other. Cassie had no idea what was going on. She wanted to ask about the text message, but she couldn't. She wouldn't. He had to be the one to bring up the whole . . . *whatever* it was that happened between him and Danica.

"So the contest was actually pretty tough," he began as he raked his fingers through his hair. "I ended up placing third," he added, in a voice almost too quiet for Cassie to hear.

"Third? That's awesome!" Cassie shrieked. It was no use even attempting at playing it cool. She couldn't help herself. The joy just sort of bubbled up out of her. She remembered how excited she had been after her first few big wins. Not that she didn't get excited with her more recent victories—the early ones just had an extra sweetness about them.

Micah's smile returned to its previous altitude. "Thanks."

"I wish I could have been there." Again, the words just sort of shoved their way out of her mouth.

What was wrong with her? How was Micah supposed to explain himself if she kept moving her mouth?

Stupid, stupid lips. It didn't help that she kept focusing on his. And that, in spite of her hurt and confusion, she still had an urge to kiss the guy.

"Hey, listen." Micah suddenly looked all awkward again.

Uh-oh. Ice water seemed to shoot through Cassie's veins. Here it came. The big breakup. Only . . . could it even be called that? Were they ever technically together?

"I'm glad I ran into you because . . ."

Everything seemed to go slow-motion. Micah's forehead went wavy again. He bit his lower lip. There was no trace of a smile.

She watched as his hand slowly slipped into the pocket of his trunks, and then . . .

A scream sounded behind her, followed by cries of alarm. Cassie spun around in time to see Tori's surfboard going airborne and her legs disappearing into a huge, crashing wave.

"No!" she cried. Oh no, oh no, oh no! Why hadn't she been paying attention?

Cassie dove off her board and swam as fast as she could in the direction of Tori's fall. This was bad. The wave looked pretty powerful. What if the current held Tori under too long? What if it knocked her hard against the floor of the sea?

The ocean was a dangerous place. Cassie should have known that better than anyone.

She lifted her head, searching frantically for signs of Tori.

"Do you see her?" It was Micah, swimming up behind her.

"No!" she answered shakily. Would she have to head into the deep surf to get her? *Could* she? Would her body even let her? Already her joints were starting to lock and her breath came in quick, shallow gasps.

Right then she spotted her. Tori bobbed up in the foamy—and not-so-deep—surf. The current, thank god, must have pushed her several yards toward shore.

Tori's hair was all in her face and her eyes were closed. Was she even conscious?

Cassie didn't waste time trying to figure it out. She swam toward her cousin, stretching her arms as far as they could reach and kicking her legs as fast as they could go.

All of a sudden, just when she was about to

reach Tori, a figure cut in front of her in the water. Hunky Surfer Guy was coming in to rescue Tori.

Cassie watched him scoop her up with one arm and then followed close behind as he side-stroked back to shore.

"Please be okay. Please be okay," Cassie chanted as they hit shallow water and ran toward the beach.

Surfer Guy gently laid Tori on the sand and bent over her.

"Let me see her!" Cassie shoved him out of the way. There was no time to be polite. Tori might need rescue breathing, and Cassie was CPR trained.

She knelt beside Tori's limp form and bent over her. "Tor?"

Tori's eyes fluttered open and fixed on Cassie. Then a tiny smile appeared and her left eye gave a quick wink.

Cassie could breathe again. She was fine! She was going to be okay!

Although . . . Cassie just might kill her later.

Micah paced about outside the whitewashed

lumber cabin that served as the camp infirmary. He wished he had something to do.

He wasn't even sure how much time had passed since he, Cassie, and some kid named Wesley had brought Tori over here. Wesley had been the one to pull her out of the surf and had insisted on carrying her all the way to the clinic. It seemed like Tori could walk the distance, but you never know with these things. Just a tiny bit of inhaled water could put the body in distress. And the force of the wave could have bounced her head off the ocean floor.

Better to be safe than sorry. He shouldn't leave until he knew for sure she was all right.

Of course, if he wanted to be entirely honest, he'd admit that Tori wasn't the main reason he was there. Truth was, he wanted to be there for Cassie. He was worried about her. And now that he'd finally tracked her down, he didn't want to let her out of his sight.

It had been such a relief to see her that morning. Yesterday evening, when she hadn't come to greet him and the others, he'd wondered if she might have blown him off on purpose. But then she explained about Tori and the board.

Unless . . . that was just an excuse?

Stop it! He had to stop driving himself nuts with all this doubts. Micah pivoted about and started pacing east-west. For about the fifteenth time, his hand crept into the pocket of his shorts to make sure Cassie's present was still there. His fingers touched the smooth plastic of the press-and-seal baggie and the lumpy form of the anklet inside it.

He had just been about to give it to her when Tori wiped out. Then he'd ditched his board and swam out to help—not even thinking about the anklet. Luckily, it hadn't been lost.

Suddenly the door to the infirmary burst open and Cassie came storming out. She was marching fast and muttering to herself, and ended up passing him completely. Micah had to jog a few yards down the path to catch up with her.

"Hey!" he cried. "What's going on in there?"

Cassie stopped and faced him. "You're still here?" She seemed surprised.

"Uh, yeah. I wanted to make sure she was okay. Is she?"

"Yes." For some reason, Cassie didn't seem very happy about it.

"What's wrong?"

"She faked it!" Cassie shouted, throwing her arms in the air. Now she was the one pacing around. "Of course the wipeout was real, but the whole 'in distress' part was played up because she saw Wesley coming to save her. She put on a total show!"

"So . . . this was for a guy?"

"Yes!"

Micah couldn't help it. He busted out laughing. "Aw, man. You got to admit that's creative."

Cassie mouth fell open as if in shock. "How can you not be mad? She freaked everyone out. And she put all of us in danger!"

"Yeah. I guess you're right," Micah said, getting ahold of his chuckles. "But come on. We've all done stuff like that. People do stupid, sneaky things when they like someone."

"*Sneaky* things?" Cassie's voice was low but full of heat. She looked as if he'd just smacked her across the face. Her cheeks had turned bright pink and her eyes flashed like blue bonfires.

Micah got the feeling he'd said the absolute worst thing ever.

"*Augh*! It's so not fair!" she shouted. Her arms

went stiff by her sides and her hands balled up into fists. "I really hate all this game playing. Why can't people just be straight with each other? Why do they have to do . . . *sneaky* stuff?"

Micah stood there, speechless. He'd only been trying to make her feel better. But somehow he'd mucked it all up.

It was clear she was mad at him. But why? What exactly did he say to set her off like that?

Suddenly Micah felt his own surge of anger. Who was she to talk about game playing? He was the one who had to track her down after he got back from Oahu. She supposedly liked him, but she couldn't leave off surfing with her cousin long enough to welcome him back?

"Hey, wait a second . . ." he started to say.

Only he didn't get to finish. Because right at that moment the camp nurse, Mona, came out of the infirmary and walked right up to Cassie.

"Good, you haven't left yet," she said. "Could you come with me to the office? I need to call Tori's parents, and I'm sure it would be a comfort if you could be there to reassure them she's okay."

"Sure." Cassie held her hurt stare on Micah for a

couple of seconds before turning toward the opposite trail. "I'll be glad to tell them the *truth*."

All he could do was step out of the path and let them walk past.

Eight

Cassie hung up the phone and rested her head on the fake wooden top of the desk. Her aunt had talked for thirty straight minutes. Of course, she had been worried about Tori. That took the first ten. The next twenty minutes were spent talking about the weather, a great trunk show at Niemans, and the fact that Tori forgot to pack the special hand cream she'd bought her.

Cassie could tell where Tori got her chatty personality.

"You okay?"

She turned around to see Charlie in the doorway. Poor guy. She'd practically taken over his work zone.

"Yeah. Just . . . bad day."

"I heard about Tori. Saw the nurse walking

159

back to the infirmary. She said she'd be all right?"

"Yeah." Cassie stood up and stretched. "In fact, she's feeling pretty good right now." *Now that she's gotten Wesley's attention*, she added silently.

"By the way, do you think we need to schedule another dance planning meeting?"

"Probably not. Did those girls give Simona the grocery list?"

Charlie nodded. "This morning."

"You've got the music taken care of?"

Again he nodded.

"Then I don't think so. We've got volunteers to set up and clean up. I really can't think of anything else . . . can you?" Cassie felt a rush of panic. She could have been overlooking something important. Something vital to the success of a dance. And she was too lame to realize it.

"No. I guess we're done." Charlie walked past her and plopped into the desk chair she'd just vacated. Then he leaned back with a melancholy gaze at the ceiling.

Looking at his sad puppy dog face, Cassie suddenly understood why he'd wanted to call another meeting. He needed some excuse to see Andi again.

"You should talk to her, Charlie," Cassie said.

"What?" Charlie almost toppled over completely.

"Andi. Just go up to her and be totally honest. Tell her you like her and you want to take her to the dance."

"Just like that, huh?" he said with a sarcastic chuckle. "No big deal."

"I mean it. I'm a girl. It's what I would want." She thought about Micah. How he almost kissed her . . . and then started sending his ex-girlfriend supersweet, private text messages. If she could stop one guy from doing all that stupid game playing, she would have done her part to help girls everywhere.

Charlie sat quietly for a moment. Soon he started nodding, slowly at first, then gathering speed. "You're right. I know you're right. But . . ."

"No buts. Do it."

At that very moment Cassie saw a familiar figure rushing down the path outside. Rust-colored, bouncy curls. Super-straight posture. Andi.

It had to be a sign!

"Here's your chance, Charlie." Cassie rushed to

the door and yanked it open. "Andi! Andi, can you come here a sec?"

"Wha? Huh? But . . ." Charlie had turned the color of loose-leaf paper. His head turned this way and that, as if desperately searching the cabin for an emergency exit.

Andi changed her trajectory without slowing down. Within seconds she was breezing into the room. "Yeah? What is it, guys?"

"Charlie wanted to ask you something." Cassie gestured toward him.

"Okay, sure." Andi turned toward him and smiled. "What is it?"

"I . . . I was . . ." Charlie suddenly looked sunburned. "I wanted to know if . . . if you wanted the Gnarls Barkley version of 'Gone Daddy Gone' or the original one for the dance mix."

"Oh. Either one. I like both."

Cassie felt both mad and sad for him. "Anything else?" she prompted.

"No. That's it." Charlie stared down at the floor, his shoulders slouched as if in defeat. "Thanks, Andi."

"No prob," she squeaked. Then, in one quick motion, she turned about and breezed out of the door.

"Please don't start," Charlie said to his shoes—only Cassie knew he was talking to her. "I just couldn't do it. I don't know why. I just couldn't. Not . . . yet."

"It's all right," she replied. "Believe me. I understand."

"Has someone been using my cell phone?" Danica looked down at her BlackBerry. Something was weird. It was on a brand-new ring setting. And she'd found it on the nightstand between her and Sasha's beds.

She *never* put it there. Sasha was her friend, but she was also the world's biggest klutz. She'd seen her knock five things off that stand in the first week alone.

No one replied. Everyone was too busy chatting about the dance and holding up dresses and shoes.

"I *said*," she repeated in a louder voice, "has someone been using my cell phone?"

"Not me," said Sierra. "Why would I use it?"

"Maybe if your phone was broken?" Sasha suggested.

Sierra tossed a peach-colored sundress onto her bed and huffed at Sasha. "I wasn't actually asking for reasons why I would use Danica's phone. I wouldn't. Even if mine was busted."

"I bet you would," Sasha pouted.

Danica rolled her eyes. Her friends were loyal and usually pretty fun. But sometimes she dreamed of knocking their heads together.

"For the last time . . . *who's been messing with my phone*?"

This time the place fell silent. Everybody stared at her, then at one another.

"Not me."

"Me either."

"I didn't."

Danica listened to the chorus of denials and scrutinized each of the faces. They all seemed to be telling the truth, as far as she could tell.

Almost all of them . . .

Not everyone responded. Across the room she could see Cassie sitting on her bed, her nose in an issue of *Surfer*. Only she didn't seem to be reading. Her posture was too stiff and unless she needed granny glasses, the magazine was a bit too close to her face. It looked more like she was trying to hide behind it.

Danica flipped open her cell and started pushing random buttons, hoping to find a clue—or at least change it back to her preset John Mayer ringtone. Let's see . . . tools? Alerts? Messaging?

Wait a sec . . . what was this?

She distinctly remembered having cleared all her messages before leaving for Oahu. Yet according to the menu she had one text saved. Even more intriguing—it had been sent yesterday, while she was gone.

"Okay. Now I *know* one of you is lying," she announced. "Who's been looking at my messages?" She held up her phone as proof.

Once again, the room got quiet.

"How do you know someone looked at your texts?" Sasha asked.

"Because I left it here when I went to Oahu. Now I find there's a saved message that I never saw. From yesterday."

"That's low," Sierra said, all open-mouthed with shock. "Why would someone get into your messages?"

"Because they're a lowlife freak, *duh*," Danica replied.

"Well, it wasn't me." Sasha looked accusingly at Sierra.

"Well, me either!" Sierra huffed. "I thought she took it with her to Oahu."

Again, Danica glanced over at Cassie. Her nose was still buried in that magazine. Was it her imagination? Or were the girl's ears turning pink?

Cassie must have sensed she was being watched. Just then, she glanced up, caught Danica's eye, and quickly looked away. After pretending to stretch she returned to her "reading," looking even more uncomfortable than before. Her bent left leg started to jiggle and her ears went from rosy pink to a dark bloodred.

Hmmm, Danica thought. *Could it be?*

She opened the file.

"It's from Micah!" Danica exclaimed. "Someone read my personal text from Micah!"

The girls gasped.

"Really? What does it say?" Sasha asked.

"Um, *hello*?" Sierra said, jabbing Sasha with an empty hanger. "It's personal! Like she said."

Once again Danica stared at Cassie, who obviously seemed to know she was being watched. The girl kept shielding herself behind the magazine, pulling in her legs and bending her arms, as if she were trying to make herself smaller.

Caught you, Danica thought. But why would Surf Girl do that? What was she up to? She was certainly acting weirder than usual.

Danica turned away from the others and read the text. It was typical Micah in all his niceness, checking up on her after her mini freak-out over losing her heat. No big deal. Then she read it again—only this time she tried to imagine herself as Cassie.

Thx for before . . . hair clip in my room . . . sneak it to you later . . .

Suddenly it all made sense. Cassie, that scheming little witch, had read her text message and assumed she and Micah had gotten all cozy during the trip! *Ha!* Served her right!

After a moment or two of power-fidgeting, Cassie suddenly jumped to her feet and started walking toward the door, accidentally knocking into Sierra, who was posing with yet another sundress.

"Hey!" Sierra cried.

"Sorry," Cassie muttered. "Gotta go . . . um . . . I left some stuff on the beach."

Ducking her head, she spun back around and flew out the door.

"Spaz," Sierra grumbled, going back to her mini fashion show.

Danica smiled. She suddenly felt a new surge of energy—something she hadn't experienced since before the surf contest.

Ever since she got back from Oahu she'd been spending all her free time "resting up" from the trip. In part because she did feel like a lazy blob, but also to avoid the endless questions her friends were dying to ask her. She'd been in the middle of one of these "breathers" when she noticed the phone in its new spot.

Now she felt better. *Much* better.

She should have felt sorry for Cassie. But she didn't.

She should have explained. But she wouldn't.

Instead she saw it as a sign.

Maybe this was supposed to happen. Maybe this was how she could finally get her mojo back.

Cassie was beginning to think there were sharks on land as well as in the deep.

First Micah and that text. And the way he'd practically admitted his vacation love match with Danica outside the infirmary. (He'd even used the word *sneaky*!)

Then Tori and her I'll-do-anything-for-a-guy-even-risk-my-own-neck-and-those-of-my-friends philosophy.

Now it seemed even her own bunkhouse wasn't safe from predators.

She lay on her bed in the semi-darkness, watching through her eyelashes as Danica held court with her friends.

"What do you mean?" Sasha urged in a whisper so shrill, she might as well have been screaming. "What do you mean the surf contest wasn't your top priority?"

"Duh, Sasha!" Sierra didn't even try to hold her voice down. "She means guys! Right, Dan? So who'd you meet?"

"Meet? Who says I met anyone?" Danica hugged her bent legs to her chest and smiled smugly. "What's the point of meeting guys when you're there with the hottest of them all?"

"You mean . . . ?" Sasha went speechless.

"Are you guys back together?" Sierra finished.

Danica lifted her right shoulder coyly. "Well . . . let's just say that I can describe the inside of his hotel room to you."

Sasha and Sierra gasped in unison. Then Sierra leaned toward Danica and said in her not-really-a-whisper, "But I thought he was with . . ." She tilted her head toward Cassie—who hoped she was doing a good enough job of pretending to be asleep.

Danica shrugged her shoulders in an exaggerated way and they all burst into laughter.

Cassie wished they would just go to sleep already. She'd tried her best to avoid this. She'd made some lame excuse to leave the cabin earlier and then wandered around like a lost kitten until it was past lights-out.

At least now she knew for certain. Her fears had officially been confirmed. Not that it hurt any less.

"He almost wouldn't leave me alone," Danica went on. "Even when we had to be apart, he kept checking up on me. Not that I minded."

Okay. I get it. You won him back. Bully for

you. Now shut up already! Cassie's gut was twisting into various knots. If it was this bad now, how awful would it feel when he officially broke up with her? She couldn't avoid that forever.

That was probably what he was trying to do that morning—before Tori's wipeout. He did seem kind of squirmy. And why else would he hang around the infirmary? Sure he was worried about Tori. But he could have gone back and waited for word. Even Wesley didn't hang around that long.

". . . and we even snuggled up in the taxi van," Danica went on. "He fell asleep resting his head against me. It was so cute."

Pleasepleasepleasepleaseplease stop! Cassie urged silently. If there were any powers in the universe that cared about her, they would strike Danica mute this instant. Or strike Cassie deaf. Or blast some harmless sleeping gas into the cabin.

And then suddenly relief *did* come. An ethereal vision that looked surprisingly like Simona filled the doorway.

"Cassie! Come with me!" the vision said.

It was Simona. Wearing a nightgown and an angry snarl, but a vision nonetheless.

"Coming," Cassie said, sitting up and pretending to yawn. She could feel all non-sleeping eyes on her as she stepped outside and joined Simona on the wooden stoop.

"You have a phone call in the office," Simona muttered. She turned and tramped down the stairs.

Cassie followed, somewhat tentatively. "Is it my mom?"

"I don't know who he is, but please tell him there are no phone calls allowed past nine unless it's an emergency."

Him? "Yes, ma'am."

During the entire walk to the office Cassie tried to imagine who it could be. Her dad? Uncle Douglas? Barry, the pool cleaner? She didn't know that many men.

It was both an utter relief to be out of the bunkhouse and a total scare that there could be bad news waiting for her.

"Line one," Simona said as they entered the office. She pointed at the boxy phone with the blinking lights. "Please turn out the lights when you leave."

Cassie waited until Simona stepped through the door to her living quarters and closed it behind her. Then she picked up the receiver and pressed the flashing orange *Line 1* button. "Hello?"

"Hey, doll! Howzit going?"

Okay. This was odd. She had absolutely no idea who it was.

"Um . . . this is Cassie Hamilton," she said, wondering if Simona might have made a mistake. The voice started laughing.

That laugh. Where did she know that laugh from?

"I know it's you, Hot Dog. I was trying to track you down. I told the grumpy lady this was an important private matter so that she'd go fetch you. Sorry if I got you in trouble."

Hot Dog? There was only one person in the world who called her that. Because she'd out-eaten him in hot dogs. Twice.

"Bo?"

Again came the memorable laugh. "Yeah, it's me. Who'd you think it was?"

"Well . . . not you! How'd you even know I was here?"

"Your friend told me. That superpolite dude. Um . . . um . . . oh yeah! Micah."

Now she was more confused than ever. "You know Micah?"

"We met at the Junior Surf Invitational. Didn't he tell you?"

"No." *That's odd*, she thought. *Why didn't he mention it?* "But . . . we haven't seen each other much since he got back."

"Well, here's some good news. I'm coming to see you!"

"You are?"

"Yeah, I'm gonna be on the Big Island tomorrow and thought I'd stop by. Is that okay?"

Cassie thought for a moment. Was it okay? It was fine with her. She'd love to see Bo. He'd always been a fun guy and it would be a welcome break from all the drama. But more importantly, would it be okay with Simona?

Only one way to find out.

"Hang on a sec, okay, Bo?"

She set down the receiver and knocked on Simona's door.

A second later it opened wide enough to reveal the head counselor's angry, and extremely tired-looking, face. "Yeah?"

"I'm so sorry to bother you. Again. It's just . . . I was wondering. What are the rules on C.I.T.s having visitors?"

"It's up to the head counselor's discretion." Simona raised her eyebrows quizzically. "Why?"

"Well . . . my buddy Bo—he's also a pro surfer— would like to stop by sometime tomorrow. He's a great guy. Really. In fact, he was just at the Surf Invitational and met Micah."

Simona let out a long sigh. "You say you can vouch for him?"

"Yes. No problem."

There was a long pause as Simona gave her a hard stare. Finally she nodded. "I guess that would be okay. You've been a big help lately. You deserve it."

"Thank you! Thank you so much!"

"But only for two hours."

"That's fine."

"And no taking him into the girls' cabins."

"No problem. Thanks again!"

Simona shut the door.

Cassie skipped all the way back to the desk and scooped up the receiver. "Bo?"

"Yeah, Hot Dog?"

175

"It's a go!"

"See this? That was from the reefs off Bells Beach. Cut right through my wet suit. And this one I got off Oahu's North Shore two years ago. It was worth it, though."

Cassie was immensely glad that Bo had come. They'd had so much fun walking along the beach and reliving old times. She'd even challenged him to another hot dog-eating contest. This time he won.

Now he was showing off his scars for the small crowd that had built up around them during their post-lunch stroll. Tori seemed to have forgotten all about Wesley for at least an hour. And Sasha and Sierra were being especially nice to Cassie for a change. This didn't seem to go over well with Danica, but at least she had the decency to keep her distance. She sunned herself on the beach, pretending not to care. Still, Cassie had caught her frowning at them a few times.

"What about that scar?" Sierra asked, stepping

a little too close to Bo and pointing to a white mark on his hand.

"Aw, that one had nothing to do with surfing," he explained. "I got that feeding some steak to my brother's dog. Apparently he didn't know where the meat ended and my fingers began!"

The surrounding pack of girls—and a few guy fans—all laughed appreciatively.

Suddenly Bo looked over their heads and smiled. "Hey!" he shouted, waving his arm up high. "Hey, Micah!"

Cold tingles swept over Cassie. She'd forgotten they knew each other. Sort of.

She turned around and saw Micah leaning over Danica, talking to her.

Of course.

"Micah!" Bo called again.

Micah finally turned and headed toward them. Although he seemed rather reluctant. His smile looked fake and he kept glancing left, right, up, down—as if he couldn't bear to gaze directly at them.

"Hey, Bo," he said as soon as he got within range. "What are you . . . I mean . . . I didn't expect to see you here."

Bo spread out his arms. "Surprise."

Everyone laughed except for Cassie and Micah.

"Just thought I'd come check out the place," Bo explained. He reached forward, grabbed Micah's hand, and gave it a vigorous shake. "It's good to see you, dude. How's the surfing coming along?"

"Oh, well. You know. Hasn't changed much from two days ago."

Bo let out his trademark laugh and walloped Micah on the back. "Now if you need any pointers, you can always ask my girl here." He slung his arm around Cassie and pulled her in a sideways hug. "She's smokin' hot on land *and* on the water—am I right?"

Cassie rolled her eyes. She adored Bo—really. He was like . . . the big brother she always wanted. But he could be so clueless sometimes.

Like now. He didn't seem to notice how awkward Micah looked. (Probably upset that, once again, he'd have to delay dumping her.) Or how stiff she was. Or how Sierra and Sasha were about to unscrew their own necks the way they kept glancing from Bo to Cassie to Micah to Danica and back again.

"Yeah. She's a big leaguer all right," Micah murmured.

What did *that* mean? Cassie tried to peer around Bo's big beefy chest to glance at Micah and check his expression. But just then Tori stepped right up to Bo, blocking the view.

"Will you give me a surf lesson while you're here? *Please*?"

"Tor, you're supposed to take it easy," Cassie reminded her. "You had that bad wipeout yesterday."

"Hey, I don't mind," Bo said. "All the more reason for her to get back out there and face it, right?"

Cassie bit her lip. She had to admit it made sense. After all, wasn't that the whole reason *she* was here at camp? To confront her own fear of the water?

"Yeah," she said somewhat grudgingly. "I guess you're right."

"Cool! So who wants to go surfing?" Hands suddenly shot into the air. Bo laughed. "How 'bout you, Micah?"

Cassie could see him now. Micah was walking backward, shaking his head.

"Sorry. Can't. Thanks anyway."

"Aw, come on! Just a wave or two?" Bo urged.

"No. Got stuff to do. Good to see you though." Without even glancing her way, he spun around and headed into the trees.

"I'm sure I'll see you around!" Bo called after him. "At all the contests!"

Micah gave a wave without glancing back and then disappeared down the path. Cassie felt a little thud to watch him go—as if someone had just elbowed her in the ribs. But at least she could breathe a little better now. She still wasn't quite ready to face him.

"All right." Bo clapped his hands together. "Let's get the surf party started!"

"I'll go grab you a camp surfboard!" Sasha cried. She raced off down the beach.

"So Bo . . ." This time Sierra sidled up close to him. "Do you have a girlfriend?"

He laughed and shook his head. "No. No way. I mean, I love girls. And I love flirting. But absolutely no girlfriends while I'm in competition mode. It's just way too much of a distraction."

Cassie felt strangely comforted by his words.

Bo was right. Maybe the fact that things were over with Micah wasn't necessarily a bad thing in the long run. She came here to get her head on straight and find her surfing legs again—and Micah had only made that harder.

Maybe it was a good thing that it was over. Or never really began.

Nine

"Sorry about your leg, man. That must suck. Especially today with the waves so awesome."

"It's okay," Cassie said, pushing down the guilt until it was somewhere behind her spleen.

"You want me to walk myself to the rental car?"

"No, I'm fine. It's not that far," she replied, adding a bit of a limp to her step—for effect.

Once again she had told a lie. A big, fat, scaredy-baby lie.

For a split second, she had been all set to go surfing with them. She thought hitting the waves with Bo might help her—that the bond they created after competing together for so long would restore her confidence and turn her back into Old Cassie. Pro Cassie. Fearless Cassie. So she followed him into surf.

Only it didn't exactly turn out that way she'd

hoped. As soon as her legs started treading the icy depths, she started jumping at every tiny grainy particle that brushed past her. After a while, she could barely keep a hold of her board, let alone surf on it. So she told them she'd really wrenched her left tendon trying to save Tori the day before and that it was acting up.

In her defense, it was only a half lie. Her tendon truly had felt a bit strained after pushing herself so hard yesterday. But it was already better.

Luckily Bo didn't try to talk her out of leaving the water. As a fellow competitor, he understood the importance of nursing wounds to prevent them from doing more serious damage. And after a few stellar rides, he joined her on the beach until it was time for him to go.

"I'm starting to understand why you came here," Bo said. He took a deep breath and added a spin to his next couple of steps—taking in the camp surroundings. "It's really kind of . . . low key. Kinda nice after the high pressure life you've been living, huh?"

"Yeah."

"I didn't understand it before. When Micah said

you were here, I figured he was just really confused. But now I get it. You've been through a lot. You deserve a break."

Cassie didn't say anything. She knew he was referencing the shark attack and she really didn't want to discuss it any further. If she did, she might accidentally reveal that the *true* reason she was there wasn't that she needed a break so much as that she was phobic about surfing.

"After the Vans competitions I might take a small time-out myself." He stretched out his arms and circled his shoulders, as if suddenly aware of the tension inside him.

"You should."

"You are coming back, though. Right?" Bo stopped walking and stared right into her eyes. "You're gonna start competing again in the fall?"

"Of course." She hoped her face looked convincing enough.

"'Cause you know, Keely's saying she'll rock the Reef Hawaiian this year and Marnie thinks she'll steal the Roxy sponsorship away from you."

"They wish!" Cassie exclaimed, feeling a genuine rush of outrage.

Bo laughed. "That's my girl."

Cassie couldn't help but crack up, too. "You know, I'm really glad you came by," she said. "It was so good to see you."

"Me too. I miss ya, Hot Dog." He reached forward and cupped her face in his big, calloused hand. "You're the greatest chick ever." He slid his hand along the side of her head, leaned forward, and kissed her right on the curve of her cheek.

A sudden rustling sounded in the nearby brush. What the heck was that? Was someone listening?

She waited a beat, but didn't hear anything else. It was probably just a bird and she was still jumpy from treading into shark territory.

"I'd tell you to send a postcard, but I know you won't," she said, facing Bo again. "Do you even know how to write?"

He pretended to look insulted and play-socked her in the shoulder. "You should talk, Miss I'm-Going-To-Camp-And-Not-Telling-Anyone. I had to hear your news from some stranger."

"Okay, okay. Fair enough."

Bo climbed into the driver's seat of his rented Dodge Neon and grinned at her. "Next time you go off-grid, tell me about it, okay? That's what friends do."

"I know. I promise." She felt suddenly ashamed. Why didn't she tell him and her other surf pals?

Because I thought they would judge me, she answered herself. She figured they'd assume something was really wrong and freak out. And then the whole world would know something was up with her.

And maybe, just maybe, she was just a tiny bit embarrassed?

"Bye, Bo. Be careful on the road. It's not like the water, you know. It hurts extra bad if you go crashing."

"Yes, Mom!" He rolled his eyes and started the engine.

Cassie stood and waved until he'd vanished around the curve.

Bo was a goofball, but he was a decent guy. And it was nice to see someone from that part of her life. Someone who only knew her as a fearless athlete and amazing hot-dog scarfer.

She might not be as daring as he thought, but at least he'd made her realize one thing: If she wanted to get back into competition mode, she needed to avoid relationships completely.

At least now there was one thing she wasn't afraid of. She was now ready to face Micah and hear his bad news.

Micah was not eavesdropping.

Not really.

Well, maybe a little.

It wasn't his fault that Simona sent him to the toolshed to fetch those garland lights for the dance. It also wasn't his fault that he had to pass right by the parking lot to get there. And it certainly wasn't his fault that Bo and Cassie were whispering sweet nothings and smooching so loudly that he couldn't help but overhear.

(Of course, he did scurry away like a scared rabbit. That was kind of a guilty-looking thing to do.)

No, he didn't need to feel ashamed about anything. In fact, he should feel fortunate that he'd witnessed Cassie and Bo's little love session. At least now he knew she hadn't been straight with him. All this time and she'd never mentioned her pro-tour romance? Did she somehow forget that she had a big, muscular, semi-famous boyfriend? God, what a fool he'd been!

Yep, it was good luck that he was walking past them at that specific moment in time. At least now he knew she was a liar.

Just like it was *bad* luck that right at this moment, on his way back to the mess hall, his path happened to merge with the path to the parking lot. And that Cassie happened to be on it.

At first Cassie didn't see him. She looked lost in thought. Probably all dreamy from kissing Superstar Bo. Finally she noticed him and her face lost all traces of dreaminess.

She came to a dead stop—possibly from surprise, possibly to let him veer ahead of her. Only . . . he also came to a halt at the same time.

So there they were. Staring stupidly at each other. Afraid to move.

Micah nervously shifted the cardboard box of lights to his right arm. Maybe if she noticed his burden she would skip on ahead, realizing he couldn't keep up.

Instead she walked *toward* him. "Hi," she said. It sounded forceful. Like a command instead of a greeting.

"Hi." His was more like a moan.

"Listen," she said, taking yet another step his way. "I've been thinking. I have to keep my head in competition mode right now. And I don't need any distractions."

Her words came out rapid-fire, as if she were scared he might run off before she finished.

Micah's body went cold. He could tell what was coming. In fact, he'd been expecting it.

"So anyway," she continued. "I think it's probably best if—"

"I get it," he interrupted. He couldn't help it. His mouth just sort of fired up all by itself. "You don't need to waste any more time on someone like me."

His anger was loud and obvious. Of course he was mad. She was a liar and a fake. But he was also mad at himself. Who was he fooling thinking she would be interested in him when she could have some superhero type like Bo?

Cassie seemed startled. "What do you mean 'someone like you'?"

"I mean, I know I'm not in your league. I realize I'm not one of these hotshot shredder guys you're used to."

Cassie looked completely taken aback. Her eyes widened and her mouth froze in an oval shape, but with no sound coming out. Probably shocked that he had her so figured out.

Since she wasn't talking, he kept on going. "It's obvious you have a thing for surfers. That's understandable. Maybe I had your interest for a while, being the top guy here and all, but then I only came in third at the surf invitational and Bo called you back up. So I've been written off for someone better. Fine. Whatever. Let's just move on."

Cassie's face turned red and blotchy. "You think I . . . ?" She stopped, cutting off her words as if strangled. Then she took a step toward him, her eyes flashing angrily. "I can't believe you! What kind of a snob do you think I am?" she shouted. "Do you really think I judge people based on their surfing skills? Or are you just looking for *a way out*?"

Micah blinked in surprise. She seemed a lot more upset than he thought she'd be. They say the truth hurts. Maybe she just didn't like the way he saw through her so fast.

"I thought I knew you!" she went on. "I thought you were . . . better than this!"

"Yeah well, I thought I knew you, too!" he snapped back. "I thought you were all sweet and special. I thought you were honest! I thought you . . ." He stopped, unable to say . . . *cared about me*.

For a moment neither of them spoke. They just listened to the shushing sounds of the wind, the waves, and the traffic on the nearby road. It seemed to Micah like the entire world was weary.

"This is too hard." Cassie shut her eyes and her voice took on a sad quality. "And it shouldn't be hard, right? I mean, if we can't even talk about stuff—if we can't even trust each other—then yeah, what's the point? Maybe we were just a big mistake." Her eyes opened. "Do you think we were a mistake?"

"Ahem."

Micah jumped at the noise. Even Cassie looked freaked. Turning around, they could now see Danica stepping out of the shadow of a banyan tree.

"Sorry to interrupt," she said. Micah could tell she was trying to sound innocent. "Simona sent me to look for you, Micah. She really needs your help stringing up the lights for tomorrow's dance. She's waiting in the mess hall, and she seems kind of grumpy."

"Okay, okay. I'm coming," he muttered, not even trying to hide his annoyance. He turned back toward Cassie only to find she had gone, her final question left hanging in the air.

Like a string of tiny lights.

So that's it. It's over.

Cassie could feel something building in her chest, pushing upward until her throat felt blocked and tears coated her eyes. How could Micah say those things about her? Did he really see her that way? As a surf-obsessed, arrogant brat?

Her first relationship ever and all she had to show for it was one canceled kiss and one awful argument.

He was so mad at her. He even said she wasn't honest. Did that mean he knew about her reading the text? She'd been wondering whether Danica had figured it out or not. Maybe she had, and had told Micah.

You really blew it, Cass, she told herself. *Big-time.*

"Whatever," she said shakily. "It's better like this, anyway. I need to focus on surfing—not him. Especially if he can't keep away from Danica."

Once again it was her head versus her body. Her brain was convinced that pulling away from Micah was the right thing to do. But the rest of her—all the soft squishy stuff inside her—was in total revolt. Tears were slipping down her cheeks and her heart seemed to be writhing around in agony.

"Yep, it's better this way," she said again, this time with a little more feeling behind it.

It didn't help.

She trudged toward the C.I.T. bunkhouse feeling absurdly tired and heavy, as if she'd somehow gained a great deal of weight in the past few hours. And considering how many hot dogs she'd eaten with Bo, it wasn't entirely impossible.

At least she wasn't hungry for dinner. She really didn't want to go to the mess hall and see Micah hanging up those lights.

As she reached her cabin, she stopped and scowled at the steps. Suddenly she didn't want to go up. What if Danica was in there acting all smug and triumphant? Even if she wasn't around, the place was probably full of happy, chatty girls busy modeling their outfits for the next day's dance.

But . . . where was she supposed to go instead?

Just then she heard a noise—a long mournful note. Spinning around she caught sight of a figure amid the hammocks strung in the nearby trees. Charlie?

The sound came again. It *was* Charlie, heaving a heavy and very sad-sounding sigh.

Cassie quickly wiped her cheeks and made her way toward him.

He was balanced on the very edge of one hammock, which caused the back side to flip up around him like a woven cage. He turned in slow half circles—creaking to the left and right and back again. As soon as he saw her he stopped.

"Hey," he greeted, somewhat unenthusiastically.

"Hey there," she said, also in a dull tone.

"You okay?"

"Yeah," she replied, trying to control the tremor in her voice. "Just . . . bad night."

"Tell me about it." Charlie blew out his breath again.

"What's up?" she asked.

"Nothing."

"Ah. So . . . want to tell me about nothing?"

He sighed again and dug the toes of his sandals in the dirt.

"It's Andi, isn't it?"

Charlie looked at her. "No. Well . . . yeah. But no." He let out an exasperated grunt and shook his head. "I mean . . . it sorta is, but really it's me. I'm the one with the problem. I just can't talk to her."

Cassie wrinkled up her brow. "Why not? Andi's sweet."

"I know that, but . . ." Again with the long sigh. If he wasn't careful, Charlie was going to pass out from lack of oxygen.

"But what?" she prompted.

"I can't get her to stop."

"Huh?"

"Just what I said. I can't get her to stop and talk to me."

Cassie perched herself on the hammock to his left and he angled his body to face her.

"See," he began. "I've thought about what you and Tori said at the meeting, and you're right. So all day today I've been trying to ask Andi to the dance. Only . . ."

"She won't stop?"

Charlie nodded glumly. "At breakfast I tried to catch her and she just said 'hi,' slammed down a yogurt drink, and headed out the door. Later on I saw her coming up from the beach, so I called to her. She said, 'Hey, Charlie,' and zoomed right past me. Then, just a few minutes ago, I finally saw her sitting down. Like on an actual bench—in the mess hall. I walked right up to her and she said, 'Charlie, did you finish mixing the music for the dance?' I said yes and she went, 'Great! Thanks!' Then she jumped up, squeezed my elbow, and sped away."

"Sounds like Andi," Cassie remarked. "I think the girl has wheels instead of feet."

"I'm giving up. She's so not interested in me."

"But you don't know that for sure!"

Charlie shot her a "get real" expression in the

dim light. "If she liked me, she would at least slow down around me. Right?"

Cassie didn't know what to say. He was making some sense. "But . . . that's still a guess. You shouldn't just assume that's how she feels. Why do people do that? Why do they just decide things about another person without bothering to ask them?"

There was a short silence. Finally Charlie cleared his throat. "Well in my case it's because I *can't* ask her. Because she's goes from zero to sixty in a matter of seconds."

Cassie cracked up. It felt good to laugh. Her insides stopped thrashing around—at least for a short while.

"But . . . I get the feeling you were actually talking about someone else?" Charlie smiled at her. A warm, sympathetic grin.

"Oh my God that's so *funny*!" A familiar voice echoed through the trees followed by a high-pitched giggle.

Tori was coming down the nearby path, hanging on a guy's arm.

"Isn't that your cousin?" Charlie asked.

"Yep."

"Is she doing okay after her wipeout?"

"She's great. As you can tell. In fact that's the guy who . . ." Cassie paused. She took a second, closer look at Tori's escort. It wasn't Wesley. This guy was shorter, with straight dark hair and not as deep a tan.

It was Eddie. Tori's ex.

"What the . . . ?"

She watched as Eddie leaned into Tori, murmured something in her ear that brought on another round of giggles, and then slowly ambled off in the direction of the guys' bunkhouses.

"Excuse me," Cassie said to Charlie.

She hopped off her hammock and caught up with Tori just as she was turning toward her cabin.

"Hey," Cassie called out.

"Cassie!" Tori lit up with one of her superwide grins. "What are you doing here?"

"Doesn't matter. What are you doing flirting with him? I thought you were over that guy."

"Well . . . I was but . . ."

"But what? What about Wesley? Remember? The guy who pulled you out of the ocean? Who saved your life?"

Tori looked down at her feet. "Wesley is great and all but . . . I'm just not sure about him anymore."

"Why not?"

"It's just . . . after all we went through with him saving me and stuff, I thought for sure he'd ask me to the Tiki Dance. But instead he wants to go on some big fishing expedition. *Fishing!* Can you believe that?"

"So you ran back to Eddie? Just like that?"

Tori shrugged. "Not exactly. I was taking a walk to let off some steam and just sort of ran into him. And he seemed so glad to see me. And well . . ." She smiled sheepishly. "I might have let it slip that I wasn't going to the dance with anyone. And he might have asked me."

"I don't believe this! You're actually going to blow off a guy—a guy you literally risked your neck for—because of some *dance*?"

"I don't know. I haven't answered Eddie yet. I don't want to mess things up with Wesley but . . . I really want to go to the dance."

"So go by yourself."

"But that's lame!"

"Thank you very much—I don't have a date. I guess I'm lame then, huh?"

Tori paused for a second, processing the information. "But you're you. I'm *me*. I kind of have a reputation to keep up."

"Seems like you're worried about your reputation in a totally wrong way."

"What's with you? Why do you care so much?" Tori crossed her arms angrily. "First you get in my face at the infirmary the other day, and now this. You're my cousin, Cassie. Not my mother!" She spun about and started stomping off in the direction of her bunkhouse.

Cassie let out a long, Charlie-type sigh. "Wait!" she called, jogging to catch up with Tori. "Look, I'm sorry. I know I'm being a big pain. It's just . . . I hate all this game playing. Nothing makes sense, you know? Why can't it make sense—at least a little bit?"

Tori shrugged. "I don't know, Cass. That's just how it is."

Cassie nodded sadly.

"But hey." Tori smiled and socked her lightly on the shoulder. "That doesn't mean you can't knock 'em dead at the dance tomorrow. Let me help you choose an outfit. *Please*?"

"No way. I'm not going."

"But you have to. Simona said all C.I.T.s and counselors have to be there to work it and help chaperone."

"Great," Cassie groaned. "Fine. Whatever. At least I can dance with Charlie. He doesn't have a date either."

"What? You mean he never asked Andi?"

Cassie shook her head.

"Well, we'll just have to do something about that." Tori turned her entire body to face Cassie. "Speaking of relationships . . . Have you had your talk with Micah yet?"

"You could say that. I mean, I know it's over for sure. I ran into him just now and he was so different. He was all angry and mean. He tried to make me out to be some big snob." Her voice cracked as she felt the pain all over again.

"Pig!" Tori growled. "Probably trying to make himself look better. So did you demand to know what was up with Danica? Did you make him squirm?"

"Well . . . I did kind of raise my voice." Cassie uttered it as if it were a question.

Tori folded her arms across her chest and shook her head. "Not good enough. Come on, Cass. There's, like, a limited time opportunity here. Trust me. You'll feel much better."

Cassie knew she was right. She did deserve reasons why he'd suddenly transformed into a cold jerk.

Only . . . she wasn't totally sure she wanted to hear them.

Ten

"And I looked all over the place. On the beach. In the water. I'm talking everywhere. And then this morning he comes over and says, 'Is this your shoe?' And he had it! Then he asked me to the dance!" Sasha hopped up and down happily, making the end of the tablecloth she was holding wave up and down like a flag.

"Omigosh! That's totally like Cinderella!" Sierra exclaimed, struggling to hold on to the other end of the fluttering tablecloth. "Don't you think so, Danica? Just like in the books?"

Danica shrugged. "I guess so. Unless this guy actually stole the shoe as a lame excuse to go find her and look like a hero."

Sasha looked as if all the air was coming out of her. Even the tablecloth drooped. "I didn't think of that. Do you think he could have done that, Sierra?"

"I don't know. Maybe. But hey, at least you have a date," Sierra grumbled.

Danica lay back on the picnic table she was sitting on—totally not caring if she messed up their perfectly aligned tablecloth. She was kind of glad she'd sucked some of the joy out of Sasha's big happy spaz attack. It was like Sierra said. Unlike the two of them, at least the girl got asked to the dance—even if it was by Henry, that geek of a first-year C.I.T.

And Cinderella? Please! How sad could you get?

Danica had never ever believed in fairy tales. Even as a little girl, she thought they were stupid.

Cinderella should have hitchhiked out of that place long before the stupid ball.

Beauties never fall for Beasts unless they have a private jet and a Swiss bank account.

And if a pea can turn some princess black-and-blue through fifty feather mattresses, that girl has some sort of rare skin disorder.

"So, I still don't get why you and Micah aren't going to the dance together," Sierra said.

Danica bristled. *Because he's lame*, she grumbled inwardly.

Out loud she said, "Because it's just a dumb dance. And besides, even though we had fun together on the trip, that doesn't mean I'm his girlfriend. I haven't decided whether I want him back or not. I'm keeping my options open."

"At least you have options," Sierra pouted. "I so need a boyfriend."

Danica ignored her and stared up at the cheesy lights on the ceiling. Why hadn't Micah asked her? It was so stupid. He and Cassie obviously weren't together, so what was stopping him?

She almost threw herself at him yesterday, after hearing him and Cassie break up. But she didn't. Micah had to come to her. That was the whole point. She didn't want to win him just because Cassie lost him. Instead, she wanted him to want her. She wanted him to come running up and beg her to take him back—which she would do. Probably.

But at least Cassie did lose him. That, at least, was an awesome thing.

The sound of the screen door opening made Danica sit up. Speak of the she-devil. It was Cassie and that annoying cousin of hers. Cassie was walking backward into the mess hall holding up one end of a large box while Tori held the other end and steered them forward.

"What's all that?" Sasha asked.

"Food," Cassie replied. "Some mini sandwiches. Fruit. Lots of hors d'oeuvre things."

"Snacky stuff," Tori explained.

They shuffled over to a long table on the other side of the "dance floor" and set it down. Danica noticed Cassie sneak her a quick glance.

"So Cassie," Sierra began in a not-so-matter-of-fact tone. "Are you bringing Bo to the dance? Or . . . someone else?"

"No, Bo's just a friend," Cassie replied. "I'm going by myself." She held her head high, but her eyes were downcast.

She looked so . . . defeated.

Danica smiled. Now that she really thought about it, she had every reason to be feeling good right now. Cassie wasn't with Micah, which meant she was back in her proper place. And it meant Micah was free. Which meant any day now he'd be coming back to her—possibly even tonight.

She lay back on the table again. The sun was setting and the lights Micah had strung up across the ceiling made it look as if they were underneath the night sky. In fact, if she squinted her eyes just a little, they really did look like stars.

For just a moment she could almost see why people wanted to believe in fairy tales.

Almost.

Cassie suddenly remembered something important: She didn't like dances.

They were just so . . . so . . . *so*.

Everybody always got dressed up and excited, like they thought some magical thing was going to happen. Then they showed up and realized that their date was rude or annoying (if they even have a date), that the music and food sucked, and that they would much rather be back at home watching reruns of *Buffy*.

Or at least that's how every dance Cassie went to ended up—all one and a half of them.

She still thought Micah was a big jerk, but at

least he'd been nice enough not to come with Danica tonight and rub it in her face. Were they not together? Or were they standing on opposite ends of the room for her sake? Somehow she doubted Danica would go along with that.

But whatever. She didn't care. At least, she shouldn't have.

"Hey, Cassie," Ben said, walking up next to her. "What are you doing stuck here? That's just wrong."

"It's not so bad." She didn't want to tell him that she was thankful to have been given the job of guarding the food table. It meant she wasn't out there trying to fake as if she were having fun while waiting for someone to ask her to dance. Plus it partially blocked her view of Micah, who was hanging with Zeke and Charlie by the music table. "How's your stomach?"

"Much better." He grabbed a handful of mini quiches and piled them on his plate.

"Hey! Everyone has a three snack minimum until 9 P.M. Can't you read?" She pointed to the sign Simona herself had hand-lettered. "The counselors want to make sure *some people* don't hog it all before everyone's had a chance to get some."

"Aw, come on. I've got to make up for lost meals, you know." He flashed Cassie his most obvious aren't-I-cute smile and reached for a mini pineapple-and-ham pizza.

Cassie whapped his knuckles.

"Ouch!" He stared back up at her, astonished. "Did you just slap my hand?"

"You already got more than your allotted three. Keep moving."

Still looking shocked, Ben shuffled away.

Great. Suddenly she had become one of those mean lunch ladies from her old elementary school. All she needed was a hairnet and orthopedic shoes.

Now she was not only having a horrible time, she was making sure other people didn't enjoy themselves either.

"Hi." Tori trudged up beside her and sighed.

"Having fun?" Cassie asked, trying to sound upbeat.

Tori rolled her eyes in her best "have you lost your mind?" expression.

Cassie felt a twinge of guilt. Maybe she shouldn't have come down so hard on the girl yesterday. It wasn't any of her business whether her cousin went to the dance with her ex-boyfriend or not. If Tori had said yes to Eddie, maybe she'd be having a good time right now. One of them should be.

"So . . ." Cassie racked her brain for a safe topic of conversation. "When should we go talk to Charlie?"

Tori wrinkled up her nose. "What do you mean?"

"You said we should help him. Remember?"

"Sure. But I'm thinking we need a new approach. I'm thinking we need to start working on Andi." Tori pointed across the room. Andi's curls were sticking out up above a small crowd of people.

"Oh no. No, no, no." Cassie shook her head vigorously. "We can't tell Andi that Charlie likes her. That's so . . . middle school."

"I'm not going to do that! I just think that, if Charlie's too much of a wuss to approach her, maybe Andi could go to him. Maybe that way she'd actually stay put a while and not zoom off. Plus it would give him confidence."

Cassie had to admit Tori had a point. The guy did need a boost.

It was odd how much she cared about Charlie's

obsession with Andi. Sure, Charlie was a pal, but that wasn't the only reason she wanted to help him. It was like . . . she needed to see someone nice have a victory in the whole romance department. She needed to believe that magic could happen for the late bloomers and inexperienced people. Like her.

"So . . . how do we get Andi to walk over to him?" Tori asked.

Cassie made a face. "Don't ask me! I'm worse than Charlie when it comes to relationships, remember?" All of a sudden tears clouded her vision. Stupid, stupid. And here she'd been doing such a good job of keeping it together.

She stared at a nearby wall, trying not to blink, hoping the tears would evaporate before anyone noticed.

"Hey." Tori gave her elbow a supportive squeeze. "Don't be so hard on yourself."

"I'm fine," Cassie lied. "Really."

Tori's eyes bored into her. "So I noticed Micah showed up alone."

"So?"

"So . . . is it possible you've got it wrong and he's not back together with Danica?"

"No way."

"How can you be so sure if you've never even asked? You've got to talk to him and nail down the truth, if for no other reason than to get some closure." Again Tori's stare seemed to dig right into her. "It will help."

Cassie sighed. *Closure*. She hated that word. It sounded so final. "You know, Tor, I don't understand why you think I need closure so badly. You're the one who keeps running back to flirt with your ex. You're not exactly a poster girl for good-byes."

Tori quickly looked down at her hands, which were fumbling with the hibiscus-patterned plastic tablecloth. "I know. But hey. At least I didn't come with him tonight. This is the very first time I've gone to a dance by myself. It's, like, historic."

Cassie's mind filled with sarcastic comments, but she managed to stop them from flying out of her mouth. She was proud of her cousin for making that decision. Besides, Tori had been a real friend lately.

"And anyway, I like being able to dance with lots of guys instead of just one," Tori went on. "You should try it."

"Maybe." *Not*.

"Attention, everyone!" Zeke had stepped into the middle of the dance floor and was now shouting through his cupped hands. "Attention!"

Gradually people stopped talking and stared at him.

"It's now time to start the limbo contest!" he announced. "Everyone please line up to demonstrate your limbo skills!"

Several cheers and just as many boos echoed through the mess hall.

"Limbo contest?" Cassie exclaimed. "We never discussed that at the meeting."

Right at that moment, Charlie walked past. Cassie reached out and grabbed his arm. "We never planned this, did we?"

"Aw, well. You know. It's tradition," he said with a shrug. "Let's just see what happens." He flashed her a shifty smile and headed off toward the dance floor.

Hmm. There was something different about him—something hidden but strong. Like a riptide.

"Come on, Cassie! Let's do the contest!" Tori tugged on her left arm.

"No. I can't. I've got to stay and work the table." Cassie tried to look a little disappointed. Truth was, she was sick of game playing and competitions. Plus, she wasn't sure her sundress would hold up. It was old—something her mother made her pack. "But you go. I'll cheer from here."

"Okay. If you're sure. But save some of those snacky things, 'kay?"

Cassie tried to look busy as the entire camp moved toward the other end of the room where Zeke and Haydee were holding up a pole. She really felt like an outsider now.

One by one, everyone bent backward under the pole. The first to fall down was big strong Ben— which made her laugh. He looked hilarious. Lower and lower the pole went. Soon more people lost their balance. Guys who clowned around too much, girls who feared the structural integrity of their outfits might give way (one of Cassie's own fears). Each time the person fell, he or she would laugh and scramble back onto his or her feet to claps and cheers.

Cassie was beginning to regret staying out of it. So what if it was just a lame game. These people were willing to risk looking stupid in order to have fun— to fully take part in life. Meanwhile she rearranged finger food.

Would she always be afraid of getting hurt?

After a while she couldn't even watch the contest. The pole was too low and the crowd had swarmed in superclose. Eventually she heard a gigantic cheer and everyone started to scatter.

Tori ran up, grinning gigantically.

"Did you win?" Cassie asked.

"No, Charlie did!"

"Charlie?"

"Yeah. That guy is amazingly limber. Who knew? Guess everyone is good at something."

Cassie felt that was true. Too bad she was too scared to do what she was good at anymore.

"Man, Charlie was, like, superhuman! There he is. See?" Tori pointed across the room. "He's over by Zeke, holding his trophy."

"And he's about to get another one. Look."

The girls stood close together, nudging each other with excitement, as they watched Andi stroll up to Charlie and give him a congratulatory hug. *Now* Charlie looked like he might lose his balance.

"Oh, I can't stand it!" Tori squealed. "This is so awesome!"

Maybe it was the thrill of his win. Or maybe

the limbo caused most of his blood to run into his head and make him dopey. But for whatever reason, Charlie managed to set down his trophy, grab Andi's hand, and pull her onto the dance floor.

And judging from Andi's face, she wasn't going to speed away anytime soon.

Cassie smiled. Score one for the nice guys.

"Why did I come here?" Micah mumbled to no one.

This dance was like torture. There was Cassie looking amazing in that soft blue dress that showed off her eyes and fluttered about her legs. The second he saw her he had an overwhelming urge to scoop her up and kiss her. Then his brain caught up with the rest of him.

It was over. They'd never get that kiss after all. Besides, she had Bo.

He wished it hadn't ended the way it did. He would have liked to have stayed friends—to have her in his life some way. But he messed things up too much. Half the time he couldn't talk to her, and when he could, he said all the wrong things.

"Hey there."

Danica walked up beside him. He noticed her lipstick matched her dark red wraparound top. For some reason it bothered him. She was so much prettier without it. Why did girls hide their looks behind makeup?

"Hi," he said, forcing himself to stop staring at her lips.

"Can you believe Charlie?"

Micah grinned. "That was really cool. I was there this morning when he asked Simona about a limbo contest. At first I wasn't sure why he'd be all into it. Now I know. The guy has secret moves!"

"Speaking of moves . . ." Danica raised an eyebrow and grabbed his hands. "Come dance with me." She tugged him toward the dance floor.

"I don't know, Dan," he protested. "I'm kind of out of it right now." But he was too weak and depressed to fully resist. The next thing he knew, he was underneath the lights he'd hung crisscrossed from the rafters.

"Even more reason," she countered, turning him to face her. "You need to make yourself have some fun." She placed his hands onto her waist and hooked her hands around his neck. "Now sway."

Micah had to smile. Danica always had a way of making him do things.

"See?" she whispered after a while. "Not so bad, is it?"

"No," he had to admit.

"This is nice, right?"

"Yeah."

She leaned back against his arms. " 'Thank you, Danica'?" she prompted with a wry grin.

He laughed. "Thank you, Danica. I'm feeling a little better now." And it was true. He was.

"You know . . ." she stopped swaying and cocked her head as if in thought. "We had a great time together last summer. Didn't we?"

"Yeah. Last summer was a blast."

"Much better than this summer. Right?"

He shrugged. "I don't know. This summer has definitely had some high points. We won the surf contest . . . I got third at the invitational . . ."

"I know, I know. Yeah, that stuff was cool and all," Danica said, nodding somewhat impatiently. "I mean . . . campwise. *People*wise, last summer totally has this one beat."

He scrunched up his nose in confusion. "You think so?"

"Well, yeah. You have to admit there's been some serious weirdness this year."

"Yeah." He glanced over to where Cassie was manning the food table. "I guess you're right."

Danica nestled in even closer, pressing her left cheek against his. "Don't you ever wish you could just . . . go back?" she whispered in his ear. The vibrations shot through him and for a second he felt an old, familiar longing.

Suddenly he could see what was coming. Danica's eyes closed and her darkly painted lips opened slightly.

She was coming in for a kiss.

He knew it would be nice. It might have even made sense in a way. But it wouldn't have been right.

Because he would have been thinking about someone else.

"Dan, stop," he said, pulling his head back slightly.

Her eyes opened and widened. "What?" She seemed totally confused. Hurt even.

"You're great. We're great—as friends. But for anything else we're just . . . wrong. We're done."

He watched as her emerald green eyes slowly iced over. "I *know* that. I'm just having some fun." She furrowed her brow. "I mean, it's not like I want you back or anything. Who said I even wanted you that way?"

"Okay," he said slowly.

"It's a *dance*, Micah. We're *dancing*." She leaned back into him and started swaying mechanically.

Micah wanted to ask when dancing involved mouths coming together, but didn't. He was just too tired. Too confused. Too scared of saying the wrong thing to the wrong person.

Danica lowered her eyes and snuggled back up against him. "You're a nice guy, Micah," she mumbled against his chest. "Maybe too nice."

"Uh . . . okay," he said, chuckling awkwardly.

"Thanks, by the way, for checking up on me on Oahu."

"Of course. No problem."

"You know, I could have won that surf contest."

"I know."

"I wasn't totally focused on it. I guess I didn't . . . want it enough," she went on. "I guess I had my mind on other things. But next time I'll really set my sights on winning, and no one will be able to stop me."

"I don't doubt it," he said with a smile. He meant it, too. Danica had more force than a crashing wave when she went after something.

He glanced over at the food table and caught a quick glimpse of Cassie serving treats to a group of kids from the *pueo* bunk.

If only he could be that focused with the things he wanted . . .

"You need to stop beating yourself up about the wipeout," he said, making himself focus on Danica again. "Winning isn't everything, you know."

She stopped swaying and looked up at him. "That's where you're wrong, Mr. Nice Guy. Winning is *everything*."

Micah sat on the steps of his bunkhouse. He didn't want to turn in yet, so instead he was enjoying the night sky and reliving the events of the past couple of days.

Man, everything could change so fast. In an instant. *Bam!* Just like a wipeout. Only with less warning.

Everything was jumbled. It was like those sliding puzzle games where you put the lion's head on the giraffe's body. He felt mismatched the exact same way.

Like . . . why was Danica making a play for him when Cassie was the one he wanted? Danica was great and all, but it could never work between them. They were too different. Danica *had* to be on top at everything. In fact, she probably only wanted Micah now because she wanted to be back at the top of his list. After all, she was the one who'd broken up the relationship last summer. Not him.

And then there was Cassie . . . how could he be so mad at her and still want to kiss her so badly? Nothing made sense.

A crunching noise made him look up. Charlie was walking down the gravel path toward him, only he wasn't exactly traveling in a straight line. He seemed to be lost in thought and would wander to the left, then to the right. Eventually he made it to the steps of the cabin.

"Hey," Micah greeted. "Howzit going?"

"Yeah . . ." Charlie half-spoke, half-exhaled. He sat down on the step beside Micah and turned toward him. "I'm sorry . . . what did you say?"

Micah laughed. "Man, where have you been?"

"Walking Andi to her bunkhouse," Charlie replied, smiling. It was an enormous smile that gleamed in the starlight. Micah got the impression only major surgery could remove it from Charlie's face.

Had he looked like that when he was flipped out over Cassie?

"Dude, you are seriously gone." Micah shook his head and chuckled. "I guess things are going pretty good, huh?"

"Life is so amazing and wonderful," Charlie said. He leaned back on the steps and tucked his arms underneath his head. It couldn't have been comfortable at all, but Charlie looked as if he were lounging back on a cloud.

"I guess," Micah mumbled. He didn't want to ruin the moment by telling Charlie he'd just been thinking the exact opposite.

Charlie seemed to snap out of his reverie. He sat back up and turned toward Micah. His brow was furrowed, but his mouth still wore a hint of a smile. "Hey man. What's going on between you and Cassie?"

Micah let out a grunt. He wasn't sure he wanted to talk about it. "Nothing," he muttered, yanking a thin sliver of wood off the railing. "Not anymore. We kind of had a thing going, but . . . stuff happened."

"So you guys broke up?"

"I guess. Yeah. Well . . . in a sense. I'm not sure if we were ever officially together. Everything went wrong so fast. She totally conned me."

"*Cassie* did? What do you mean?"

"I mean, she wasn't up-front with stuff. She, like, set me up. I thought she was so cool, but she wasn't."

"Huh." Charlie nodded in a way that showed he wasn't convinced. "But . . . if you guys weren't all on the record as a couple, how could she have gone behind your back and stuff? I mean, how could she break the rules if you hadn't given her any?"

Micah couldn't reply. He'd never really thought of it that way.

"Cassie doesn't seem like the sneaky, dishonest type," Charlie went on. "Maybe whatever happened, she had a good reason for it?"

Micah scoffed. "How should I know?"

"Well, I'm no expert but . . . maybe you could try asking her."

Eleven

Cassie felt like a backward Cinderella.

She'd been to the stupid ball, but now here she was sweeping up, feeling sorry for herself.

Not that she minded sweeping. In fact, she'd volunteered to clean up after the dance. And she'd already shooed off Charlie so he could walk Andi back to her bunkhouse. She hoped it would give him more time with her, plus she just wanted to be alone.

And she was in no hurry to go back to her cabin and overhear Danica talk about Micah.

It was odd. The two of them didn't seem to be together at the start of the dance. Then later she caught them looking really cozy on the dance floor.

But Danica or not, Cassie and Micah were obviously wrong for each other. It hurt bad enough discovering that he'd blown her off for his ex-girlfriend. And yet hearing him accuse her of being a surf snob was worse. It meant he didn't get her at all. That he obviously never did.

Cassie let out a grunt as she pushed aside one of the tables in order to get to the crumbs underneath. It actually felt good to be active after standing behind the snack table for three hours. When she was done cleaning, she'd promised to take out the trash for Charlie. Then maybe she'd take down the lights for Zeke and Micah so they wouldn't have to do it in the morning. Then maybe she'd scrape the walls and repaint . . .

Anything to keep herself occupied.

The screen door suddenly opened and in breezed Tori, her face lit up like a jack-o'-lantern. "Cassie! You'll never believe it!" she exclaimed.

"What?"

"Look! Look what Wesley brought me back from his fishing trip." She held out her hand. In it was a perfect, pristine sunrise shell.

"Wow."

"Do you know how rare these are?"

"Yeah. They're like the diamonds of seashells."

"I know!" Tori cradled it against her face.

"Please don't tell me this means you're engaged."

Tori laughed. "No. But I'm so glad I didn't go to the dance with Eddie and louse things up with Wesley. Thanks for that. For setting me straight."

Cassie smirked.

"No, really. I know you think I'm, like, this expert on relationships, and I do act like it sometimes. But I'm not. No one is."

"Whatever," Cassie said, feeling awkward. "You're better than I am anyway."

"Don't sell yourself short. I mean, so what if you don't have loads of experience. You're smart. And honest. And just a really awesome person. You deserve the best and you'll get it." Tori reached out and caught Cassie up in a long and slightly suffocating hug.

Cassie didn't know what to say. Her cousin usually wasn't the type for a Lifetime Network moment.

"What I'm trying to say is . . . maybe you shouldn't come to me for advice," Tori went on, releasing her from her embrace. "People like me play games because we're afraid of just telling the truth. You're not and that's awesome. So don't start the games. Okay?"

"Okay." Cassie said, unsure of how else to respond.

"So . . ." Tori clapped her hands together, as if breaking a spell. "Can I help you clean up?"

"No, thanks," Cassie said, waving her off. "It's after curfew and Simona would freak if she knew you were out of your cabin. Besides, I've got it under control."

"Well, okay. See you in the morning." Tori stared down at the sunrise shell as she headed for the door. "I really need to figure out how to make some jewelry out of this."

Cassie shook her head and chuckled, watching as Tori disappeared into the darkness.

She had just bent down with the dust pan when she heard the screen door open again. "What now?" she called out. "Forget to tell me something?"

"Yeah. Lots of things," came a familiar voice.

Only it wasn't Tori's voice.

Cassie slowly stood and turned around. Standing just inside the entrance was Micah, his eyes sagging sadly. In his hands was a beautiful yellow wildflower.

"Uh . . . hi," she said.

"Hi." He stepped forward and held out the blossom. "This is for you. I'm pretty sure it's custom for a guy to give flowers when he takes a girl to a dance."

"Um . . ." Cassie scrunched her brow in confusion. "But I think it's customary to take the girl to the dance before the dance is over."

"Who says it's over?" He walked up to her and pressed the flower into her hands. "Feel like dancing?"

Cassie felt like she'd entered some bizarre dream. It was all so wonderful, but it made no sense. "Uh . . . there's no music," she pointed out.

He smiled. "Sure there is." He gestured to the iPod hooked onto his shorts. Then he pulled out a pair of earbuds. One he put into his right ear. The other he pushed gently into her left. Suddenly she could hear a smooth-voiced man singing a moody ballad. Usher, maybe?

"Shall we?" Micah asked, lifting his arms.

Again Cassie had the distinct impression that

she'd entered some sort of Neverland. She wouldn't have been surprised if a mermaid came flopping into the room.

She wasn't Cinderella. She was Alice in Wonderland.

"Sure," she finally replied. Tucking the flower behind her right ear, she stepped into his arms and rested her head against his chest.

At first it was awkward. Her feet kept bumping into his and he kept shifting his hold as if uncomfortable.

Finally, they found that perfect fit. And there they stood, gently swaying. She could smell the ocean on his shirt and feel the flutter of his heart beating. It was easy. It was nice.

What is this? she wondered. *What does this mean?*

She wished the voice inside her would shut up. It was ruining the mood. Why did it have to mean anything? Friends could dance. Maybe this was Micah's way of saying that they didn't have to hate each other just because they couldn't be a couple.

Perhaps he read her thoughts because all of a sudden he stiffened slightly and cleared his throat.

"Hey, uh . . . I'm sorry about before," he mumbled. "Sorry I jumped to conclusions about you and Bo. I guess I was just jealous."

Cassie tried not to smile. "It's okay," she replied, trying to match his somber tone.

"No, it isn't. I had no right. I mean . . . we never really said we were a couple. You know, like, all exclusive. Right? So how could I get mad at you seeing an old boyfriend?"

Cassie let out a snort. *"Boyfriend?* No way. Bo's just a buddy."

"Oh." She glanced up in time to see Micah grin ever so slightly.

"But I know what you mean." This time it was her turn to get all serious-sounding. "We didn't make things clear beforehand. I mean, obviously we weren't all exclusive or you and Danica wouldn't have hooked up during the trip."

Micah stopped swaying and took a step back. "What? Who told you that?"

The shock in his voice surprised her. Suddenly she realized she was going to have to make a small confession. "Well . . . no one. I sort of accidentally saw your text to her." She could feel her cheeks turning color. "But . . . it's okay. I mean, I understand how things can get between exes. Kind of. And like you said, we weren't serious."

"Wait, wait, wait." Micah was shaking his head. "I'm lost. What text? What did it say?"

"You were thanking her . . . for something . . . she'd left her hair thing in your room . . . you were going to *sneak* it to her." She winced at the way she emphasized sneak.

After all, it was pretty sneaky of her to have read the text.

Micah wore a look of total astonishment. "What were you doing reading Danica's te—" He shook his head and cut himself off, much to Cassie's relief. Finally he gave a nod. "Okay. I guess I could see how you would be worried. But it didn't mean what you thought it meant. Danica wiped out hard in her first heat and went back to the hotel without her key. I went to check on her and let her calm down in our room. That's all."

"Oh."

She wasn't in dreamland anymore. She'd been yanked back into reality. The ache in her chest proved that. So did the creases in Micah's forehead.

"I thought you knew me better than that," he said.

"I'm sorry," she mumbled. All at once she felt a surge of indignation. "But you should have known me better, too. When you thought I was with Bo. When you thought I judged guys by their surfing skills."

He hung his head. "Yeah, you're right. Sorry."

They stood there for a long moment, listening to the guy on the iPod sing about finding someone in his dreams.

Eventually Micah gave her a shy smile. "So . . . maybe it just means we need to get to know each other better?"

Cassie grinned back at him. "Definitely. I just wish . . ."

"What?"

"I still wish it wasn't so hard. All this should be easier, right?"

Micah shook his head. "I don't think so. To me it should be like . . . surfing. Surfing is freaking hard—at least at first. But if you really want it, you stick with it. Pretty soon it gets easier. And it's so worth it. Even when it's difficult."

"Yeah." Cassie could understand that.

Suddenly things made a little more sense. Even the music sounded better and the world seemed a little brighter.

She was in the real world and it was a wonderful place.

"Hey, um . . . I was scared to do this before but . . . I have something for you." Micah reached into his pocket and pulled out a small plastic bag. "Sorry. Didn't have time to wrap it or anything." He opened the bag and lifted out a beautiful braided anklet with tiny seashells in the shape of a flower.

"Ohhhh! It's beautiful!" she exclaimed, holding it up to the light.

"Really? You like it? I was scared you'd think it was . . ."

"I love it! It's awesome."

"*You're* awesome."

Cassie's eyes met his. They were sparkling under the overhead lights. As she gazed, they came closer and closer. Then they closed completely.

She shut her eyes, too, and let other senses take over. She could feel the warmth of his breath, the feel of his hands on her back. And then . . .

. . . his lips were on hers. They were kissing.

235

It was soft and yet not soft. Sweet but not too sweet. Scary but not too scary. It was real and amazing and right.

Time passed in some magical, immeasurable way. At some point, the earbud popped out and everything went silent, except for the sounds of the crashing surf. Or maybe that was her breathing.

Eventually, they pulled apart.

"So . . . just to be clear," he said. "We're together? Exclusively? Just the two of us?"

"Just us two," she said, smiling.

"Good." He grinned back at her. "And now to make it official. Will you allow me?" He took the anklet out of her hand and dropped down on one knee.

Cassie held out her right foot. Once again she felt a little like Cinderella—a modern, tropical, super low-key version. Without all the cheesy Disney music.

"There," he said. He rose to his feet and leaned in for another time-bending kiss.

I have a boyfriend! Cassie marveled at the thought.

No, even better: I have Micah.

236

Okay, so maybe she wouldn't follow Bo's lead after all. A relationship could be a good thing instead of a distraction, right? After all, she was afraid of getting hurt by Micah and now that fear had been overcome.

And if she could overcome this fear, maybe she could conquer her other one, too.

Summer CONFIDENTIAL

TWILIGHT

"Sorry I'm late," he said to Cassie. "One of the guys in my bunk thought it'd be funny to pull the plug to my alarm clock." Lame, but true.

"Don't worry about it," Cassie said casually and without a hint of sarcasm. "Tori and I were here chillin', watching the waves." Her eyes sparkled when she smiled at him.

"Nice," Micah said, thinking how cool it was that Cassie was so laid-back about it. If it were Danica standing there, she'd give him her typical icy glare, followed by an all-day guilt trip, ending with an argument. Not wanting to seem like a complete hound, Micah figured he should probably say something to Cassie's cousin. "'Sup, Tori?"

Tori removed her sunglasses. "Hey."

It was then when Micah noticed that the area

around Tori's eyes was pale but the regions above and below them were a blotchy bright pink. "Dude, what happened to your *face*?" he asked her.

"Nothing." Tori glanced warily at Cassie, then immediately removed the mini compact she had sticking out of the side of her bikini bottoms. She opened it and gasped at her reflection. "Oh, no! We came out before sunrise and I forgot to put on my Stila SPF 45!" she cried, inspecting her sunburned face at all angles. "I'm hideous!" She turned to Cassie. "Why didn't you *tell* me I was burning? You know my skin is supersensitive—like a baby's bottom."

"You mean you have diaper rash on your face?" Micah joked, and Tori cut him a dirty look.

"Sorry, Tor. I didn't notice it, I swear." Cassie took her cousin's chin in her hand. "Let me see."

"Ow!"

"It's not so bad. I'll bet you could, you know, even it out with a little makeup?" Cassie suggested.

"Oh, God. You think?" she said sarcastically, then stomped up the path toward her bunk. "Carlie, Tasha! Get me my bronzer, quick!"

Cassie turned to Micah. "I think she's peeved."

Do not laugh, Micah thought, watching Tori scurry away in her platform sandals. *Do not laugh at Cassie's cousin. Do . . . not . . .*

On the fifth second he cracked, "Bahahahahahahah!"

"Stop! It's . . . not . . . funny!" Cassie said, but she was giggling now, too.

A few short minutes later, they'd caught their breath and were left with a slightly awkward silence. Normally this would be Micah's cue to lean in and kiss her again—a more meaningful kiss—but he held back.

If it were anyone else he might have just gone for it, right then and there, but this was Cassie. He didn't want to plant one on her because they didn't know what to talk about. Plus, after all the drama it took for them to finally get together, officially, he wasn't sure if a bold move would freak her out.

In short, he needed a sign.